#4

The Inn at Holiday Bay
Answers in the Attic

by

Kathi Daley

D1520134

This book is a work of fiction. Names, characters, places, and incidents either are products of the author's imagination or are used fictitiously. Any resemblance to actual events or locales or persons, living or dead, is entirely coincidental.

I want to thank the very talented Jessica Fischer for the cover art.

I so appreciate Bruce Curran, who is always ready and willing to answer my cyber questions; Jayme Maness for helping out with the book clubs; and Peggy Hyndman for helping sleuth out those pesky typos.

And, of course, thanks to the readers and bloggers in my life, who make doing what I do possible.

Thank you to Randy Ladenheim-Gil for the editing.

And finally, I want to thank my husband Ken for allowing me time to write by taking care of everything else.

Books by Kathi Daley
Come for the murder, stay for the romance

Zoe Donovan Cozy Mystery:
Halloween Hijinks
The Trouble With Turkeys
Christmas Crazy
Cupid's Curse
Big Bunny Bump-off
Beach Blanket Barbie
Maui Madness
Derby Divas
Haunted Hamlet
Turkeys, Tuxes, and Tabbies
Christmas Cozy
Alaskan Alliance
Matrimony Meltdown
Soul Surrender
Heavenly Honeymoon
Hopscotch Homicide
Ghostly Graveyard
Santa Sleuth
Shamrock Shenanigans
Kitten Kaboodle
Costume Catastrophe
Candy Cane Caper
Holiday Hangover
Easter Escapade
Camp Carter
Trick or Treason
Reindeer Roundup
Hippity Hoppity Homicide

Firework Fiasco
Henderson House
Holiday Hostage
Lunacy Lake
Celtic Christmas – *December 2019*

Zimmerman Academy The New Normal
Zimmerman Academy New Beginnings
Ashton Falls Cozy Cookbook

Tj Jensen Paradise Lake Mysteries:

Pumpkins in Paradise
Snowmen in Paradise
Bikinis in Paradise
Christmas in Paradise
Puppies in Paradise
Halloween in Paradise
Treasure in Paradise
Fireworks in Paradise
Beaches in Paradise
Thanksgiving in Paradise – *Fall 2019*

Writers' Retreat Mystery:

First Case
Second Look
Third Strike
Fourth Victim
Fifth Night
Sixth Cabin
Seventh Chapter
Eighth Witness
Ninth Grave

Whales and Tails Cozy Mystery:

Romeow and Juliet
The Mad Catter
Grimm's Furry Tail
Much Ado About Felines
Legend of Tabby Hollow
Cat of Christmas Past
A Tale of Two Tabbies
The Great Catsby
Count Catula
The Cat of Christmas Present
A Winter's Tail
The Taming of the Tabby
Frankencat
The Cat of Christmas Future
Farewell to Felines
A Whisker in Time
The Catsgiving Feast
A Whale of a Tail – *Summer 2019*

Rescue Alaska Mystery:

Finding Justice
Finding Answers
Finding Courage
Finding Christmas
Finding Shelter – *Fall 2019*

A Tess and Tilly Mystery:

The Christmas Letter
The Valentine Mystery
The Mother's Day Mishap
The Halloween House
The Thanksgiving Trip
The Saint Paddy's Promise
The Halloween Haunting – *Fall 2019*

The Inn at Holiday Bay:

Boxes in the Basement
Letters in the Library
Message in the Mantel
Answers in the Attic
Haunting in the Hallway – *Fall 2019*

The Hathaway Sisters:

Harper
Harlow
Hayden – *Summer 2019*

Haunting by the Sea:

Homecoming by the Sea
Secrets by the Sea
Missing by the Sea
Betrayal by the Sea
Christmas by the Sea – *Winter 2019*

Sand and Sea Hawaiian Mystery:

Murder at Dolphin Bay
Murder at Sunrise Beach
Murder at the Witching Hour
Murder at Christmas
Murder at Turtle Cove
Murder at Water's Edge
Murder at Midnight
Murder at Pope Investigations – *Summer 2019*

Seacliff High Mystery:

The Secret
The Curse
The Relic
The Conspiracy
The Grudge
The Shadow
The Haunting

Road to Christmas Romance:

Road to Christmas Past

Chapter 1

I looked out my window and smiled as the bountiful days of spring pushed out the last breath of winter, bringing rebirth and renewal to the rocky seashore and dense forest. After months of short days, long nights, and frigid temperatures, the sun shone brightly, causing flowers to bloom, birds to sing, and wildlife to venture from their winter homes. In the forest, rivers spilled over their banks as the annual runoff found its way to the sea.

As I set about tidying my room, I decided that today was the day I was absolutely going to start cleaning out the attic in the mansion I'd been refurbishing to operate as a country inn. My contractor, Lonnie Parker, had been bugging my roommate, Georgia Carter, and me to get it done so that he could start ripping out walls and adding plumbing to create the last of the six suites we planned to rent to our guests. The suites on the three main floors of the mansion were just about completed and ready to be furnished. Lonnie thought the attic, once we got it cleaned out, would take six to eight weeks to complete, depending on the plumbing and electrical situation, which he couldn't confirm until he was able to open up the walls. At this point, we were looking for a completion date for the inn in mid-June. That actually worked out, because we'd all but decided to hold a grand opening celebration in July. We didn't have overnight guests booked until August, but we wanted to do a couple of outdoor events first, to ease into the whole 24-7 scenario.

I pulled up the top quilt on my four-poster bed after straightening the lower layers and was smoothing away the wrinkles when my Maine Coon cat, Rufus, attacked the pillows, messing up the quilt in the process. "Get down, you silly cat. I'll never get this done with your help."

"Meow."

"Yes, I know that you want to play, and normally, I'd be happy to play with you, but I have a very busy day planned. Let's finish making this bed and then go have some breakfast." I picked up the orange cat and then took a deep breath. "I smell coffee as well as something baking in the oven. Maybe Georgia made muffins today."

I'd already dressed in shorts and a T-shirt, so I grabbed a pair of flip-flops and slipped them on my feet. While my main goal today was to get started on the attic, I also had a crew coming by this afternoon to put the finishing touches on the float for this weekend's Easter parade. In addition to my need to tackle the attic and finish the float, I was itching to get outside in the garden, which my landscaper and I were planting if the opportunity presented itself. The landscape architect had drawn up a lush and colorful setting that would take years to grow in completely, but I figured it should be downright gorgeous right off the bat once the flower beds and planter boxes were added.

"Abby." Georgia knocked on my bedroom door just as I was tossing my overnight clothes into my laundry hamper.

"Come on in," I called out as I set Rufus on the floor.

Georgia opened the door and stepped inside. "There is a woman at the door asking to see you. She said that she went to the main house first, but Lonnie sent her over here."

I frowned as I tried to imagine who could be looking for me so early in the morning. I had workmen coming and going all the time, many of whom had a multitude of questions, so I figured maybe it was one of the subcontractors who had come to the door. "Okay. I'll be right out."

"I'll go ahead and ask her to have a seat while she waits," Georgia offered.

When I entered the living area of the two-bedroom cottage I shared with Georgia, Rufus, and Georgia's Newfoundland, Ramos, I found Georgia speaking to a petite woman with long red hair that fell almost to her waist. I smiled in greeting as I crossed the room. "I'm Abby Sullivan."

The woman stood and offered her hand. "My name is Trish Roswell." She bent down to scratch Rufus under the chin before she continued. "I'm here on a fact-finding mission of a sort. I recently had my ancestry charted as the first step in writing a family memoir and it seems that my great-great-great-aunt was Abagail Chesterton, the wife of Chamberlain Westminster, the man who built your house in 1895. I was hoping that you might know more about Abagail and would be willing to share it. I find I am very interested in the woman who won the heart of such a fascinating man."

Okay, I wasn't expecting that. I wasn't certain what I was expecting, but it wasn't someone working on a family tree. "Really?" My tone mimicked my surprise. "Abagail had a niece? I guess I should have assumed that she had family, perhaps even siblings. I know that she never had children, but I guess I never stopped to look at the situation beyond that."

Trish nodded. "My great-great-grandmother was Celeste Chesterton, Abagail's sister. Their father, William Chesterton, married Isabelle Portman in 1864. They had three daughters, Elizabeth, Abagail, and Celeste, and lived in a small coastal settlement just west of modern-day Holiday Bay. Elizabeth died when she was just twenty-four. As far as I can tell, she never married or had children, although my investigation into the Chesterton family is sketchy at best. I know that Abagail married Chamberlain Westminster when she was twenty-two. They likewise never had children. Celeste married a man named Reginald Gram in 1902. They had two sons and a daughter. The daughter, Maria, was my great-grandmother."

"And do you have children?" I wondered.

The woman nodded. "I married a wonderful man ten years ago and we have two daughters. The girls are spending some time with their grandparents over spring break, so I decided to use the time to try to fill in some blanks in my family history."

"That is so awesome." Georgia grinned. "It sounds like you have done quite a bit of work already."

"I have." The woman's bright blue eyes shone with enthusiasm. "I've been looking up distant cousins on both sides of my family and visiting the gravesites and birthplaces of those ancestors whose whereabouts I have been able to track down. When I started this journey, I tried listing everyone, including cousins and their spouses and offspring, and then I realized how many people you can collect in just a couple of generations. After the first two generations, I decided to concentrate on direct descendants, such as grandparents and their parents and siblings. I have run across a few who I found particularly interesting, including Abagail. I know that she died while living in the house on this property, although I don't know for certain where she was buried. I hoped you might know."

"Actually, I don't, but there might be folks in town who do. My contractor, Lonnie Parker, might even be aware of the details of Abagail's final burial place. We can go ask him. He knows a lot about the history of the house and its past residents."

"That would be great. If Abagail is buried close by, I'd like to pay my respects and maybe see if I can pick up any additional information for my family memoir."

"There may also be items in the attic of the main house that could answer some of your questions. Georgia and I planned to start cleaning it out today. I'd be happy to take down your contact information and call or email if we find anything we think you might be interested in."

Trish smiled. "I'd like that very much. Do you think there is anything in the attic that could have belonged to Abagail?"

I shrugged. "I have no idea. The house had six owners before me. As you already know, Chamberlain Westminster had the home built in 1895. After Abagail died, he returned to England and the house sat empty until he passed away and his brother, Simon, inherited the estate and sold it to the Joneses in 1932. To be honest, I don't know what they might have done with any personal possessions Chamberlain might have left behind. They may have sold whatever they didn't want, but I suppose it is possible they stored more personal items in the attic."

"I hope that is true," Trish said.

"When I moved in, the place was mostly cleared out, except for a few random pieces of furniture, although the attic was packed from top to bottom and front to back with boxes and furniture. Going through everything is going to be a big job, that is for certain. Georgia and I have been meaning to get to it for the past month, but spring in Holiday Bay is a busy time, with the return of tourists and local celebrations to ring in Easter, so we've managed to push back the task several times." I looked at Georgia. "Today, however, is the day. Right?"

"Right," Georgia answered.

"Like I said, I'm happy to call you if we find anything I think you might be interested in," I continued.

"I would appreciate that very much. I am in town until tomorrow, and then I'm heading to Lewiston, where a cousin of my grandfather on my father's side lives. I'll be there for several days, but if you find anything that belonged to Abagail, I'd be happy to come back here when I am done there to take a look."

"That sounds like a good plan," I responded. "In the meantime, let's go talk to Lonnie. There is a good chance he knows where Abagail is buried."

When we arrived at the main house, Lonnie was on the phone with the electrician, so I offered to give Trish a tour. I had to admit I was very proud of the way things were coming together. Everything looked so fresh and new, and the floors, as well as the countertops and new windows, glistened. The addition of the wall of windows to the back of the house where it overlooked the sea had made such a huge difference in the overall feel of the place.

"So, you have named every suite and have given each one a different color palette?" Trish commented as we walked through the five suites that were finished or mostly so.

I nodded. "Pretty much. The same dark hardwood flooring runs throughout the house. My thought was that the flooring would pull everything together in a seamless manner, despite the color variations."

"I think it does. I really like it."

"While the suites are decorated differently, they are all laid out in a similar manner. Each one has a sleeping area with a king-size bed, a bathroom with a jetted tub, and a sitting area with a fireplace and a private balcony or patio. And they all have an exceptional view of the sea."

"I noticed that the place had the feel of the sea from the moment I walked in through the back door into that fabulous kitchen," Trish said. "And I love that each suite has a name, but with a name like The

Inn at Holiday Bay, I sort of thought you would give holiday names to the suites."

"Georgia and I talked about having a Halloween Suite, a Christmas Suite, an Easter Suite, and so on, but then we realized that there might not be a huge demand for guests wanting to stay in a Christmas-themed suite in July. Besides, the town of Holiday Bay seems to cover the year-round, holiday theme pretty well. We do plan to hold seasonal and holiday events, but the theme of the suites has more to do with the color scheme of the forest and sea."

"Well, I think what you have done is truly spectacular."

By the time I had given Trish the grand tour, Lonnie had finished his conversation. I asked him if he knew where Abagail was buried and, as I suspected, he did. He also knew quite a bit about the Chesterton family, including that when Abagail passed away, she was laid to rest in a family cemetery that was located on land owned by her family. It was still there, although no one had been buried in the cemetery for quite some time. It was only about twenty miles west of Holiday Bay, so when Trish said she was going to make the trip, Georgia and I decided to go along, even if that meant putting off the attic for one more day.

I offered to drive because I pretty much knew where we were going and Trish had never been in the area before. Georgia sat in the back so that Trish could enjoy an unobstructed view.

"The Maine coastline is stunning," Trish said as we headed west. "I wish now that I had more time to spend exploring, but I have a pretty tight schedule that will need to be adhered to if I want to have the opportunity to speak to everyone on my list."

"You could always come back for a longer visit at another time," Georgia suggested. "The summers along the coast are magnificent, and of course, the fall color when the trees turn is something that everyone should experience at least once in their lives."

"I'd like to come back one day. Maybe I will bring my family. My husband has a demanding job and it is hard for him to get time off, but he usually takes a week off in the fall and another week at Christmas."

"The inn will be open beginning in August. If you can figure out dates, call us. The suites have foldout sofas, so if you don't mind having your daughters sleep in the seating area, the whole family can share one suite."

"I'll keep that in mind. I'd really love to come at Christmas. I bet the town is magical when you add snow to the rocky bluffs overlooking the sea."

Magical was exactly the way I'd describe Holiday Bay at Christmas. As much as I was happy to see the end of the snow from last winter, I was sure I'd welcome it once the holidays rolled around.

As soon as we arrived at the old homestead owned by the Chesterton family, we got out of the car and looked around. The house, a large, two-story structure, was deserted and looked as if it had been for some time. The private graveyard was bordered with a short fence measuring about three feet in height. It was mostly overgrown with weeds, but most of the headstones seemed to be intact, which would help us to identify the individuals buried there.

Trish was thrilled to find William, Isabelle, Elizabeth, Abagail, and Celeste, all buried close together. In addition to Abagail's immediate family, multiple generations of Chestertons and people who must be Chesterton relations were buried in the cemetery as well.

"I love the idea of families spending eternity together," Georgia said.

"It is pretty sobering," Trish agreed. "I'd have to bring my notes with me to be sure everyone is buried here, but based on the number of tombstones, it looks like a good percentage of the Chesterton clan ended up here."

"I wonder who this grave belongs to," I said, pointing to a grave marker next to the one identified as having belonged to Elizabeth Chesterton. "It simply says 'Emily.' There is no last name."

Trish frowned. "I'm not sure. I don't remember an Emily on my family tree, but I'll look when I have my notes."

"Maybe there was a fourth daughter in the family," I suggested.

Trish shook her head slowly. "No. I don't think there were four daughters."

"Perhaps she was a friend of the family," Georgia said. "Maybe there is a journal or old letters or something in the attic that will explain who Emily was. Are there other nonfamily members buried in the cemetery?"

I looked around. "With the exception of Emily, almost all of the grave markers have both a first and last name on them. The last name of most of the individuals buried here is Chesterton, but there are a few with the last name of Gram and Birmingham."

"Celeste married Reginald Gram," Trish said. "They had two sons and a daughter. The sons and their families would be Grams. The daughter, my great-grandmother, Maria, married Clifford Birmingham."

"It looks like the last person to be buried here was Annalisa Birmingham. She was only twelve when she died in 1942," Georgia said.

"She was the youngest daughter of Cliff and Maria, who had five children. Annalisa fell off a horse and broke her back. She died several weeks later," Trish informed us.

"That is so sad," I said, feeling the tug in my heart that only a mother who had lost a child could really understand.

"I wonder why no one else was buried in the little cemetery after that," Georgia said.

"I'm not sure," Trish said, looking around. "Until Lonnie told us of its existence, I had no idea this was even here. Maria is buried in Stowe, Vermont. I know she lived in Vermont when she died, so perhaps my great-grandparents moved after the death of their youngest child. Cliff was originally from Vermont."

"Sometimes all you can do when you lose someone you love and your life falls apart is move away and try for a fresh start," I said.

"Yeah," Georgia agreed. "That makes sense. We can research the land and find out if it was sold at around that time." Georgia blushed. "Not that I am trying to take over your project. I tend to get wrapped up in this sort of mystery."

"No, it's fine," Trish assured us. "I'm thrilled to have found someone who is interested in the project. My sisters have asked me to stop bringing it up all the time, and my mom is only mildly interested, to the point where she will listen to my stories but never offers to participate. My husband is a great guy and supports me, but I can tell that he couldn't care less about knowing where Abagail Westminster was buried."

"Not everyone is interested in digging into the past," Georgia admitted. "But I find it very interesting and would be happy to help with the research, especially the parts that involve Chamberlain Westminster and Abagail Chesterton."

"You should take her up on her offer to help," I said. "Georgia is a master on the computer."

"I will take you up on it," Trish told Georgia. "And thank you."

"I noticed that the gravesites are laid out so that the most recent are in the front, which I suppose must mean the earliest Chesterton ancestors are buried toward the back," I commented.

"Let's take a walk there and look around," Trish said. "I'd love to walk through the cemetery slowly and write down every name and the year they were born and died. It will not only help me fill some of the holes I have in my family tree, but it would be interesting to find out what I can about everyone as well." Trish looked around. "While Celeste is buried in the cemetery, as are her two sisters and her parents, I notice that only one of her children, Henry Gram, seems to have been buried here. I wonder what became of Celeste's youngest son, George."

"Perhaps George moved away and was buried elsewhere," I said.

"Perhaps," Trish agreed.

"Oh look," Georgia said from a kneeling position at the back of the graveyard. "Here is Robert Chesterton. He was born in 1774 and died in 1840. The oldest grave seems to belong to Baby Boy Chesterton, born in 1803. He was survived by his parents, Robert and Louise." Georgia looked up. "I suppose that Robert might have built this little cemetery for his baby when he passed away before he could have been named. Maybe once he was buried here, the other members of the family began to be buried here as well. Maybe to keep Baby Boy Chesterton company for all eternity."

"Wow, that is sort of poetic," Trish said. "The baby had no name, yet he left a legacy if this entire graveyard, which later had dozens of grave markers, began with his death."

This outing was most definitely bringing up issues for me. As we looked around, we found gravestones for quite a few children. I supposed that there was a time when a lot of children died at a young age. I wondered if it was as hard to lose a child back then as it was now, or if married couples simply went into it knowing that they would lose a few along the way.

We ended up spending several hours in the little cemetery. Trish noted the names of several family members she wanted to research further, including the Emily who had no last name. I wondered if perhaps she wasn't a valued servant. Maybe a nursemaid who died and was so much a part of the family that she'd earned a place in the family cemetery.

When we returned to Holiday Bay, we stopped off at Velma's Diner for lunch. Trish wanted to buy lunch for Georgia and me as a thank-you for helping her out, and I thought she'd enjoy getting to know one of the pillars of modern-day Holiday Bay.

The restaurant was packed with folks who were out and about, enjoying the warm spring weather. Georgia spotted a booth in the back and quickly headed in that direction. I grabbed a couple of menus as we passed the hostess station. Velma and her waitress were running a mile a minute, so I figured I'd save them the hassle of bringing the menus to us. Georgia and I already knew what we wanted, but I was sure that Trish would want to take a peek at the items Velma offered.

"I hoped to introduce you to Velma, but I didn't realize it would be this busy," I said to Trish. "I doubt she'll even make it out of the kitchen."

"I'm sure she must be pretty busy," Trish agreed. She glanced at the menu. "What's good?"

"Everything is good," I answered.

"Velma is known for her home-style country cooking," Georgia said. "You won't find anything fancy on the menu, but what she offers is of good quality and prepared with love."

"I guess I'll try the beef-dip sandwich," Trish said. "I haven't had one in ages."

Georgia went up to the counter, wrote down the order for our table, and slipped it to Velma. Then she grabbed three glasses, filled them with water, and brought them to us. The sole waitress on shift that day waved at Georgia to acknowledge that she'd noticed that she had taken care of things herself. That was one of the things I loved about Holiday Bay: Folks pitched in when necessary, and no one seemed to mind.

"So, how many people are you trying to meet during this family roots trip of yours?" I asked after we'd all settled in to wait for our food.

"I have seven on my list. I live in Philadelphia, but both my mother's family, as well as my father's, are from New England. I know most of the aunts, uncles, and cousins who are still alive, of course. This trip is to find additional information on the ones who came before. I have my lineage traced back to Nicolas Chesterton on my mother's side. As far as I can tell, he came to the colonies in the mid-1600s. He lived in Jamestown and had seven sons. In fact, one of the most interesting things I found was that the Chesterton line consisted mostly of sons until William Chesterton, who had three daughters."

"William Chesterton had brothers whose offspring carried on the Chesterton name?" Georgia asked.

Trish nodded. "He had two brothers."

She went on to name the brothers and their offspring. While I found it fascinating, Trish was throwing way too many names around for me to make sense of them, so I let my attention wander. Georgia seemed better able to keep up with all the names, but I felt like I would need a list to keep track. One of the bits of information Trish had stored in her memory that I did find fascinating was that one of the uncles many times removed had been named John. John had eleven sons, all of whom were named John too. I wondered how that might work, but Trish informed me that all the sons had different middle names, so she assumed that the sons went by those.

After we finished lunch, we headed back to the mansion so Trish could pick up her car. She had plans to visit both the newspaper and the museum, and Georgia and I had a whole hive of worker bees coming by to help put the finishing touches on the float for the Easter parade, so we didn't tag along. Lonnie had built a masterpiece with the help of his artistic wife, Lacy, and our neighbors, Tanner Peyton and his sister, Nikki. He'd been working for weeks on a replica of the inn, all fixed up and ready to receive guests. In addition to those helpers, we were expecting Chief of Police Colt Wilder, Velma, when she was finished at the diner for the day, and Velma's friend, Charlee Weaver.

I suggested to Georgia that she grill some burgers and buy a couple of bags of chips to serve to everyone when they arrived. Of course, once Georgia got hold of the idea, burgers on the grill translated into ribs and chicken, baked Texan beans, potato, green, and fruit salads, and fresh, flaky grilled bread. I'm not sure how Georgia got all that food prepared so quickly, but by the time Colt rolled onto the drive on his motorcycle, the meat was on the grill and everything else was ready to eat.

"I'm not sure I would have gone with quite so much food," Colt said later that afternoon after everyone had arrived. "I'm afraid we'll all end up in a food coma and no one will have the energy to work on the float."

"I agree, but you know Georgia; when I suggested hamburgers and potato chips, she almost had a heart attack. I think we'll be fine, though. There isn't a lot left to do on the float. We finished the structure as well as the basic landscaping last weekend. We wanted to add an Easter feel to the inn and garden, so we plan to build a large Easter Bunny who will sit on a chair in the gazebo, and then we'll add Easter eggs to the lawn. I think Lacy and Georgia have everything made, so it just needs to be assembled."

Colt yawned. "That's good. After the long day I've had, I could use an early night."

"Long day?" I asked.

"I spent a good part of the day moving my furniture into my new house. I still have to move the small stuff and most of the boxes, but I got a good start. I hoped to finish up tomorrow, but I got a call about human remains that were found in an unmarked grave about two hours north of here. It was too late to make the drive today, so I am heading out in the morning. Local law enforcement has the remains in their morgue, so there wasn't a lot of urgency to make the trip today.

"Why are you responding to a call so far north?"

"I think the body could be connected to a case I looked into a while back when the victim turned out to be alive."

I raised a brow. "Alive?"

"It's kind of a long story," Colt warned.

"I have time."

He took a sip of his beer and then sat down on one of the patio chairs we'd set out. I sat down next to him.

"About three years ago, I received a call in the middle of the night from a woman named Erica Kurtzpatrick. She claimed to have witnessed her neighbor, Peter Slavin, stab his wife, Lora, in the throat. I responded to the call, but when I knocked on the Slavins' door, no one answered. Because I had reason to believe that a murder may have been committed on the property, I let myself in. A quick tour of the interior of the home didn't provide evidence to support the vicious attack the neighbor swore she had witnessed, and while I carefully searched the whole place, I was unable to find even a drop of blood."

"Was there evidence of a struggle?" I asked.

"No. Likewise, there was no evidence of forced entry, and it didn't appear as if anything had been disturbed. It was the early hours of the morning by that point, so I waited to see if Peter Slavin would return to the house. When he hadn't come back by the morning, I tracked him down through his employer, who informed me that he had been attending a conference in Atlanta for several days. I called Slavin and confirmed that he had been at the conference all week. I asked him about the whereabouts of his wife and he said she had been out of town visiting a friend while he was in Atlanta. I called the cell number he provided and Mrs. Slavin answered. I informed her about the reason for my call and she agreed to a brief interview via video chat to confirm that she was indeed alive and kicking."

"Then what did you do?"

"I had zero evidence of foul play in the house and the supposed victim looked to be very much alive, so I dropped the case."

"And the neighbor?"

"I shared the information I had tracked down with her, including that I had spoken to Mrs. Slavin. Despite the evidence that she was very much alive, Erica Kurtzpatrick swore that she wasn't crazy and had seen what she said she had."

"Did you consider that while the wife was alive, the neighbor might have seen someone else being murdered?"

"It did cross my mind, but the evidence didn't support that conclusion."

"Okay, so why do you think the body that was found today is related to that case?"

"This body was that of a female wrapped in a large blue area rug. The victim had been stabbed in the throat and the victim wore pink nylon pajamas. When I spoke to Erica Kurtzpatrick three years ago, she told me that she saw her neighbor, Peter Slavin, walk into the dining room where his wife, Lora, was standing and stabbed her in the throat. When I took the report, Erica told me that she'd noticed that Lora was wearing the same pink nylon pajamas she'd seen her in on other occasions, and when I explained that I had searched the place and hadn't found a body or even any blood, she told me that Lora had a large blue area rug in the dining room and that, based on what she saw, Lora would have been standing on that rug when she was stabbed. She reasoned that the rug would have soaked up any blood that would have resulted from the stab wound and that it was likely that Peter had disposed of the rug at the same time he disposed of the body."

I raised a brow. "So how were you able to speak to Mrs. Slavin if she had, in fact, been murdered?"

"That is exactly the question I hope to answer."

Chapter 2

Georgia and I began tackling the attic the next morning. We knew it was going to take days to get through more than a hundred years' worth of keepsakes and discarded items, so while neither of us wanted to spend the day indoors, it was time we finally got started. The space was layered with decades of dust and cobwebs, making our job a dirty one for sure. It was hard to tell which of the previous owners might have left things behind, but based on the pure volume, I'd say all of them.

The plan was that we would do two passes. During the first pass, we'd set any trash or items we wanted to donate into the hallway in separate piles, and one of Lonnie's men would haul them down the stairs, throwing the trash in the dumpster and the items to be donated in the back of Lonnie's truck. We would set the things we'd already identified as worthy of being used in the house to one side, and Lonnie or one of his men would carry them downstairs and place them where we instructed them. Everything we were unsure what to do with would go in the basement for a second pass and final decision at a later date.

In the beginning, the room was so packed that there was little room to work. It made it difficult to go through the boxes, but I knew once we cleared out a space to work, things would go more smoothly. The first several boxes were full of old dishware and linens we suspected had been used when the house was a resort. Both, we decided, would go in the donation pile, although the linens might eventually end up as trash. There was a really nice rocking chair I would have Lacy refinish for the library and a buffet table that would look nice in the dining area if Lacy could stain it to match the dining table. We hadn't established a needs-to-be-refinished section, but I could see we would need one, so for now, I asked Max, one of the laborers helping us, to take those things down to the dining room and set them off to the side.

"I hope we come up with something that will help Trish find the answers she is looking for," Georgia said as she sifted through the boxes closest to where she was working.

"She does seem really into finding out everything she can about her family history. I know that the whole ancestry thing is really popular right now, but I've never had the urge to do my own."

"Yeah, me neither, but Trish did awaken a spark in me. Who knows, maybe after we get the inn open and things slow down, I'll give it a whirl. Not that I have a lot of relatives, and those I do have I haven't seen in years. I think Trish had a bit more to go on to get started. It sounds like she has grandparents, aunts, uncles, and cousins that she is in regular contact with."

"I guess that would be nice, although I never really missed having a lot of relatives in my life." I opened a box and peeked inside. "It looks like this is full of books. I'll have one of the guys take them to the library and we can sort through them later."

"This box has pool supplies," Georgia informed me. "I guess this must be left over from when the Joneses had the spa."

"Just donate it. I don't plan to put in a pool anytime soon. I just found three more boxes of books." I stood up and walked out into the hallway. "Max," I called down the stairs. I could hear two men talking on the landing just below me.

"Yes, ma'am."

"Grab a buddy and come on up. I need someone to carry several boxes of books down to the library on the second floor."

"Yes, ma'am."

At first, I was annoyed that everyone called me ma'am, which made me feel old, but I'd gotten used to it and barely even noticed it at this point.

"I have a feeling that if we are going to find anything that was left by Chamberlain or Abagail, it will be toward the back of the attic," Georgia said.

"Yeah, I was thinking the same thing."

"Do you want these dishes?" Georgia held up a white plate with a blue stripe.

"We have a lot of plates, but if you come across serving pieces, holler." I paused and reconsidered sending them directly to the donation pile. "Why don't you take a photo of them and send it to Lacy?" I suggested. "I suppose before we donate them, we should verify that they aren't valuable, one-of-a-kind antiques. In fact," I added, "I'll just text her to see if she can come over while the older kids are in school."

"That's a good idea. She can give you feedback on the items you are thinking of refinishing as well."

I called Lacy, who was happy to stop by to help out while Georgia continued to sort. After I hung up, I checked my email and messages while I had my phone out. I opened my mail app and gasped.

"What is it?" Georgia asked.

"I have an email from Annie." Annie was my sister. She still lived in San Francisco and we had not spoken in person since I'd moved to Maine. I'd tried to reach out to her by sending her chatty emails a couple of times a week, but she'd never answered. She had sent me an email letting me know that she was thinking of me when Ben's thirty-fifth birthday rolled around, but that had been the last I'd heard from her.

"What does it say?" Georgia asked, setting the box she was sorting through aside and giving me her full attention.

"I don't know. I haven't opened it yet."

Georgia sat quietly, waiting for me to set the pace.

I took a deep breath and opened the email. "My aunt Polly died," I said in a soft voice.

Georgia got up and crossed the room. She gave me a good, long hug. "I'm so sorry."

I leaned into Georgia's strength. "It's okay. We weren't close. In fact, I haven't seen her since I was eight or nine."

Georgia pulled back a bit. "Yet you seem upset."

I shrugged and tried to appear unaffected despite the fact that a single tear rolled down my cheek. "I'm sorry Polly passed away. I'm always sorry when anyone dies. She was actually my great-aunt. I think she must have been in her eighties. I remember her as being really nice, but, as I said, I haven't seen her in years. I guess I am more upset about the email."

Georgia frowned. "Why? It was nice of Annie to pass along the news."

I took a deep breath and blew it out. "I guess. It is just that the entire email is a single sentence: Aunt Polly died. I suppose I should be grateful for that much, but a sentence or two about how she is doing or even a 'Love, Annie' at the end would have been welcome."

"I don't know Annie, so I don't really know what I am talking about, but it almost seems she has erected walls she is not yet ready to let down. It feels like she is keeping you at arm's length because she is afraid of being hurt."

I paused to consider this. "You might be right. I guess I should be happy she bothered to let me know about Polly at all. I'll reply and thank her. I'll ask her if she knows if there will be a service. She might not answer, but I'll try."

Georgia stood up and brushed off her pants. "I'm going to run downstairs to see if I can get a couple of the guys to clear out what we already have in the hallway. There is a lot more that will need to be moved out and I feel like we need to make some room."

I smiled and nodded at my best friend, who knew I could use a few minutes to myself. Georgia was one of those people who could see into your heart. She always seemed to know what you needed and when you needed it. Honestly, I couldn't have asked for a better person to walk with me into my new life here in Holiday Bay.

Once I sent off the sweetest email I was able to come up with, I returned to the task at hand. I could hear Georgia talking to Max, so I figured they were on their way up the three flights of stairs. So far, all we'd found were the sort of things I'd expected to find. Not that the attic didn't possess items of value, but I was hoping to find something extraordinary. Something that would make me gasp with awe. Something that would make me wonder how such an important piece of history could go undiscovered for so long. I guess after all the other secrets this house had revealed, I'd come to expect a new secret around every corner.

"Okay, the guys are going to tackle the items we stacked for the dumpster or to donate first," Georgia informed me. "Lacy pulled up just as I headed up the stairs. She is chatting with Lonnie, but I imagine she'll come upstairs next. In addition to the box with the dishes, there is one with sewing supplies. I'm thinking it might be a donate box, but I'll have Lacy look at it first. Do you still want that secretary down in the entry?"

I nodded. "For now. I'm trying to decide between the entry and the parlor for it. I think I see a couple of old trunks in the back of the room. I'm going to try to make my way back there to see if there might be hidden treasure inside."

"A treasure chest would be fun, but personally, I'm hoping for journals or letters or artwork, perhaps. I keep hoping we'll find paintings that Chamberlain might have completed but never sold stacked away up here somewhere."

"That would be awesome," I agreed. "I really would love to have his work displayed in every room of this grand old house."

I decided that the most direct route to the chests was to clear a path by scooting boxes off to the side. They would still need to be looked through, but we could work on them later. Chances are that most of the boxes contained things that we would donate. If there was treasure, I reasoned, it would be in the trunks.

"Morning, ladies," Lacy said as she blew in through the door like a breath of fresh air. "It looks like you already have made a really good start."

"We got up early, so we've been working on it for a couple of hours already," Georgia said.

"We realized we should get your opinion on a few things before we donated them," I added. "We don't want to end up storing a lot of stuff we won't use, so if we don't have a place for it, we plan to donate it."

"With the exception of personal bits of history such as photos and old letters," Georgia amended.

"Have you found letters and old photos?" Lacy asked, opening the box with the white dishes. She lifted one out and turned it over.

"Not yet," Georgia answered. "But we are still hoping. What do you think of the dishes?"

"You can sell them to an antique store. They aren't super rare or valuable, but they are in good shape and it looks like you might have a complete set. I wouldn't donate them. If you don't want to keep them, I'll help you sell them."

"I guess we need a pile for that," Georgia said. "We are trying to sort things as we go. Keep, trash, sell, donate, etc."

"That's a good idea," Lacy agreed.

"Oh look, photos." Georgia held up a fistful of old, black-and-whites.

"Let's have the guys put the box in the cottage. We can go through them later. There might be stuff in there that Trish will be interested in as well."

"Trish?" Lacy asked.

Georgia explained who she was and what she was after. Of course, a woman on a quest to reveal her family history grabbed Lacy's attention right off the bat. *I should have thought to call her yesterday.* Lacy loved history and valued family more than anyone I had ever met.

"How far into her search is she?" Lacy asked.

"Pretty far," Georgia answered. "She knows the names and birthplaces of folks dating back to the seventeenth century. It seems she has ancestors who lived in Jamestown, but she doesn't know a lot about those relatives. It's all pretty interesting. We went with her to the cemetery where Abagail Chesterton Westminster is buried. We didn't realize Abagail had sisters until yesterday. Apparently, Trish is descended from Celeste Chesterton, the only sister to have children."

"It was pretty awesome," I jumped in. "There were grave markers dating back more than two hundred years."

"Trish had an appointment with a cousin on her dad's side yesterday afternoon, but she is going to stop back in Holiday Bay when she is done," Georgia said. "I'll introduce the two of you."

"We are hoping to find additional information about the Chesterton family up here in these boxes," I said. "I wasn't overly curious about Abagail and Chamberlain before, at least not in terms of their ancestry, but now I find I am totally drawn into their story. It was interesting to read all the grave markers and to try to imagine who those people actually were. I found myself wondering how they looked and what sorts of personalities they had. Who found love and who didn't, who lived out their lives and who died young…"

"There was one grave marker that just said 'Emily,'" Georgia informed Lacy. "Nothing else. No last name or date of birth or death or anything. I can't help but wonder who she was."

"All of the other markers had both first and last names?" Lacy asked.

Georgia nodded. "And based on the last names, Trish said that all were related to Robert Chesterton, who seemed to have established the cemetery when his infant son died. The only marker without a last name to establish the connection was Emily."

"I wonder if she was an illegitimate child," Lacy said.

"We hadn't thought of that," I said. "We did suspect she might have been a valued servant, such as a much-loved nanny."

"That explanation could work as well," Lacy agreed. She sat back on her heels. "Now I'm curious about the identity of this mysterious Emily too."

Lacy headed back downstairs to work out the transport of all the items I wanted her to refurbish for the inn. Lonnie's truck was full of items to donate, so she arranged for one of the laborers to take the items to the secondhand store to free up space for the next load. I continued to make my way back to the trunks and Georgia went on opening and sorting through each box as she came to it.

"More photos," she called and picked up a few. "I think these are from the days when the estate was used as a resort. Check out the main living area, which was used as the lobby back then." Georgia held up a photo. "The place is packed. I guess the resort was a popular place in its heyday."

"Lonnie and a few other people I have spoken to have said that the resort was popular with those seeking time in the healing waters of the pool," I responded. "It's too bad the pool was damaged in that hurricane. Based on the fact that the resort went under not all that long after that, seems to indicate it was the attraction that brought visitors here."

"The Joneses had the pool, but we'll have our luxurious suites and theme weekends," Georgia said. "I'll have the guys take this box of photos to the cottage too. There are a bunch of old bar glasses in this box." Georgia looked up. "I am assuming they are left from the resort as well. We haven't talked about having a bar, and even if we thought it was a good idea, I don't know where we'd put it. Do you want the glasses for anything?"

"No. Let's donate them. I think I can finally squeeze through and get to the trunk."

"Is it locked?" Georgia asked.

"It's latched but not locked." I slowly opened the heavy lid. "Jackpot," I said.

Georgia looked up at me. "Did you find a treasure?"

"Better. I found a trunk full of sketches by Chamberlain Westminster."

"Really?" Georgia asked with a tone of awe in her voice.

"Really. There are several dozen in a variety of sizes." I pulled out one and held it up. It was about twelve inches by twenty and featured a section of coastline that I recognized as being located about a mile down the road. This particular piece was a watercolor, but there were also pencil sketches and even a few oil paintings in the trunk.

Georgia stopped what she was doing and headed through the maze I'd created as I made my way to the trunk. She squeezed in behind me. "Wow," she said. "Just wow. I hoped we'd find a few pieces to hang in the suites, but there are enough pieces here to put at least two items in every room in the inn."

I picked up a pencil sketch. "This is the cemetery. The one we visited yesterday. Of course, only the oldest gravestones are there." I pointed to a headstone toward the front of the sketch. "This is Elizabeth Chesterton's." I pointed to the sketch. "Abagail's isn't here yet, so he must have done the sketch after Elizabeth's death but before hers."

"Which means that Emily was buried after Elizabeth's death because her headstone is near Elizabeth's and it isn't here either."

I nodded. "I guess that helps us narrow down the timeline a bit. Let's have a couple of the guys take this box to the cottage. We can sort through it later. I'm afraid if we get too distracted with these now, we'll never get the attic cleaned out." I looked toward the back of the room. "Besides, there are two more trunks to explore. I can't wait to find out what sort of treasures we'll find in them."

"Personally, I am still hoping for letters or journals. Some sort of firsthand account of life provided by those who lived in the house before it was abandoned for all those years," Georgia said.

"Letters or journals would be awesome. We can assume that Chamberlain was well educated, but I wonder about Abagail."

Georgia held up something in her hand. "I found a box with guest books."

"Guest books?" I asked.

She opened the cover. "It looks like they were placed in the rooms when the house was a resort. Guests would jot down a sentence or two about their stay." Georgia thumbed through one of the books. "Some wrote more. This guest, for example, wrote about the man she married and the honeymoon they had at the resort. It's drippy sweet but sort of heart-touching." Georgia looked up. "I wonder if it worked out for them."

I shrugged. "I hope it did. Let's have the guys take this box to the cottage as well. It will be fun to read through the entries."

"Maybe we can build a display case in the library for some of the books. They are a rather interesting piece of history."

I grinned. "Yes. Let's do that." I looked around the attic. "If a lot of these boxes have treasures, we might want to have Lonnie build us a little building off the main patio to serve as a museum. There really does seem to be a lot of history just waiting to be shared."

Chapter 3

By the time we'd managed to clear out the attic, we'd taken several loads to the second-hand store for donation and filled the dumpsters with trash twice and Lacy's workshop with items in need of refurbishing, as well as partially filled the basement with items to go through again and the small cottage with trunks and boxes holding artwork, photos, guest books, and, yes, the journals Georgia was hoping for. Trish had texted and let us know that her girls were going to be with their grandparents for an additional week, so she planned to extend her trip. She would be spending a couple more days with the cousin in Lewiston and then head back to Holiday Bay afterward. Georgia had filled her in on the photos and journals and Trish was as excited as we were to have a look. The cottage was filled to capacity with boxes we wanted to take our time to sort through, but today was Saturday, so Georgia and I planned to put everything aside for a few days so that we could enjoy the Easter parade and other holiday events.

Lonnie would be driving our float in the parade, so Georgia and I found a spot along the crowded sidewalk to watch in front of the Holiday Bay Community Bank. While the small businesses along the main thoroughfare were open today, they would all close between ten and eleven so their employees could watch the parade as well.

"I ran into Patrice Hamilton on Wednesday when I stopped in the bank to cash a check," Georgia said, referring to the widow of Jasper Hamilton, the founder of the Holiday Bay Community Bank. She didn't work there, but she was there chatting with her son, who had been the manager since her husband had died. "She said that before Jasper died, he donated cash to the summer arts program each year, but her son has decided to put an end to it."

"Did she say why?" I asked.

Georgia shook her head. "She didn't elaborate, but I could tell that she is pretty fed up with the way the bank is being run since Jasper's death. According to Velma, who, as you know, is friends with Patrice, Wesley seems to be so focused on the bottom line that he has totally forgotten the spirit of community that led Jasper to establish the bank in the first place. Velma even said that Patrice told her that Wesley has been receiving threatening emails since the new policies he established have taken effect."

"Policies such as not participating in sponsoring charitable events?"

"That and the fact that the bank has new guidelines about late payments and foreclosures." Georgia took a deep breath. "Velma told me that the number of people being kicked out of their homes and businesses has more than tripled since Wesley took over."

"And Patrice can't do anything about these new policies?"

"I guess not. According to Velma, Jasper left the bank to his son to run as he saw fit. Velma seemed to think that Patrice might donate some of her own money to select local organizations the bank had supported in the past, but while she is very wealthy, her funds aren't unlimited, so that is only a temporary solution. It's Velma's opinion that the organizations that previously depended on donations from the bank would be well served to come up with other sources of funding if they wanted to continue to do what they've done."

I stepped aside to give more room to a couple with a stroller. The parade wouldn't start for another thirty minutes, but Georgia and I were aware that if we didn't arrive early, we wouldn't end up with a good spot to watch the procession. "It seems to me that Wesley is just hurting himself. One of the reasons the people in town supported the bank was because of Jasper's commitment to give back to the community. If the bank pulls their support from organizations that they supported for years, there is going to be pushback."

"It seems that between the threatening emails and the loss of business, Wesley would reconsider, but so far, I haven't heard any chatter that would indicate that he had."

I waved to Nikki Peyton, who was walking down the opposite side of the street with her new guy friend, Jack. She waved back but didn't approach. If I had to guess, Jack and Nikki had picked up on the fact that neither Georgia nor I thought her relationship with the much older man was a good idea, so the couple was avoiding us.

"Is that Royce?" Georgia asked, pointing to a spot down the street from us.

I turned to see Velma walking toward us accompanied by a man we'd met during our recent trip to Nantucket. Royce Crawford was an old friend of Velma's who, prior to that trip, she hadn't seen in decades. The two had gone to dinner together while we were on the island, but Velma had assured us that, after their one evening of catching up, that would be the end of their reunion. Apparently, she'd been wrong.

"Royce, what a pleasant surprise," I called out as the pair approached us.

"Royce surprised me with a visit," Velma explained.

From the tone in her voice, I couldn't tell if she was happy or upset by his appearance. What she seemed was flustered. In fact, every time Royce's name had come up, Velma had seemed flustered. At the time we'd run into him, Velma had sworn that their friendship had come to an end years before, but now that I had the chance to really observe their body language, I wasn't entirely sure that was true.

"When I ran into Velma on Nantucket, she reminded me about the parade, so I decided to make the trip this year," Royce commented after he'd hugged both Georgia and me. "It looks like there is a good turnout."

"There is, and I'm glad you made it," Georgia responded. "Abby and I entered a float this year. We are excited for everyone to see it."

"I'd heard that you'd replicated the Inn at Holiday Bay. I'm looking forward to seeing what you've come up with."

"Our contractor, Lonnie Parker, did most of the work," Georgia informed him.

"But Georgia was the one who came up with the overall concept," I added.

"The best efforts tend to require teamwork." Royce smiled.

"Will you be in town long?" I asked.

"A few days."

"Where are you staying?" Georgia asked.

"Oh look, there's Charlee," Velma said, interrupting the flow of the conversation. "I should go to say hi," she added almost frantically.

Royce chuckled as Velma scooted away. "She's a skittish one, my Vel. But I tamed her once, so I'm confident I can do it again." He looked down the street. "It was lovely seeing you girls."

With that, he headed toward Velma, who seemed to be trying to lose him, judging by her erratic behavior.

"Do you think Velma is playing hard to get?" Georgia asked.

I narrowed my gaze. "I'm not sure, but it did strike me that she didn't want us talking to him. She might not know herself what she wants to do about this flash from her past."

"The chemistry between them seems to be the real thing."

I nodded. "I agree with that, but sometimes chemistry isn't enough. Sometimes once trust has been lost, it can never be regained."

I watched as Royce disappeared from sight. He was a bit too cocky for my taste, yet there was something about him that I found appealing. He had a good sense of humor and certainly seemed willing to go after what he wanted. He was strong-willed for sure, but Velma was strong-willed too, so maybe they'd be good for each other.

"By the way, I know this is totally off the subject, but seeing Royce made me think of reconciliations with those lost along the way. Did Annie ever email back to you about the service for your aunt?"

"Yes, she did," I answered. "It seems that Aunt Polly stipulated in her will that she didn't want to have a funeral of any sort. Her grandson had her remains cremated and placed next to Uncle Bill, who passed away years ago."

"I'm glad she got back to you."

I smiled. "Yeah. I will admit that I was surprised. She even asked me about the inn. I emailed back and gave her a long update, which I am sure was a lot more than she was looking for. I also invited her to the grand opening. I told her she could be our first guest and could have her choice of rooms if she came. She hasn't answered me, but I feel like I laid the groundwork. I'll ask her again after she has a chance to think it over."

"Is your sister married?"

I nodded. "She is. Her husband is one of those people pleasers, and he tends to go along with whatever she wants. I guess their relationship works for them. They seem happy. I extended the invite to both Annie and Arnie. I'd love to see them both, but we both know that it is Annie my heart is longing for."

Georgia took my hand in hers and gave it a squeeze. "Oh look," she said. "The parade is starting."

The parade was amazing. It seemed like every business in town had entered a float in the annual parade. The Inn at Holiday Bay float ended up taking second place, behind the one entered by the preschool, which I had to admit was both innovative and heartwarming.

"Should we head to the food court that has been set up in the park or would you rather just go to a restaurant?" Georgia asked once the judging was over and we had received our second-place ribbon.

"Let's hit the food court. It seems like a junk food sort of day."

"I want to try one of those pulled pork sandwiches everyone has been talking about. It sounds as if the rub used to slow cook the meat adds a unique taste that one might not expect from pork. I'm always anxious to try something new."

When we arrived at the food court, we ran into Tanner Peyton, who'd been chatting with one of his trainers. He'd just taken possession of a new litter of puppies for training, and Georgia was eager to spend some time with them. She joined their conversation while I wandered over to a table where Colt was sitting with Lacy and Lonnie and their six children.

"Second place." I handed the ribbon to Lonnie. "I'm surprised you didn't come to the awards ceremony."

"The kids were demanding to head over to the kiddie carnival, and I didn't want to leave Lacy alone with all six of them any longer than I had to." Lonnie grabbed his phone and took a photo of the ribbon. "Second place is awesome. Did the kids from the preschool take first?"

I confirmed that they had.

"I'd invite you to join us for lunch, but we're about done, and the kids want to head over to the Easter egg hunt," Lacy said.

"The egg hunt sounds like fun. Don't let me keep you. Georgia is around here somewhere with Tanner. I'll just go look for them."

"I'll stay here with you," Colt said. "I'm not sure an egg hunt is quite as alluring as a barbecue beef sandwich."

After the Parker family had gone, Colt and I got in line for sandwiches. "How is everything going?" I asked.

"It's been a busy week," he answered. "I feel like things are starting to come together at the house, but between reopening the Lora Slavin case and preparing for this weekend, I've been swamped."

"Any news on the case?"

"Not really. I still don't have confirmation that the body in the grave belonged to Lora Slavin, but I suspect it very well might. If that is true, it will give me a reason to bring Peter Slavin in for questioning, so in anticipation of receiving the results I expect, I've decided to locate him, though it seems he has disappeared."

"Disappeared?"

"He no longer lives at the residence he gave me as his forwarding address after leaving Holiday Bay three years ago. He quit his job and didn't leave a forwarding address with them either. In fact, according to his old boss, he simply stopped coming in. I checked with the DMV and found out his license expired two years ago. As far as I can tell, he hasn't renewed it in any state. I am waiting to hear back from the IRS about his federal tax returns. I'm not sure they will give me the information I am looking for without a warrant, but all I really want to know right now is whether he has filed a return in the past two years. They might tell me that much."

"The fact that he seems to have fallen off the face of the earth does seem odd. Do you think he left the country?"

"Perhaps. It's too early to tell, but if it looks like the remains in the gravesite are those of his wife and we suspect he is the killer, he is not going to be easy to track down."

Colt and I chatted about the possibilities while we ate. If the body in the grave belonged to Lora Slavin, the next logical step would be to track down the woman who had masqueraded as his wife during the phone conversation Colt had with her. Could Lora have a look-alike relative? A sister no one knew about? Even a twin? Might the woman Peter had presented as Lora have been a doppelgänger? Unlikely, but I supposed it was possible.

The other possibility was that the woman in the grave was not Lora Slavin but someone who looked like her. In a way, that seemed more likely, because the woman who was killed had been seen through a window from across the street in the middle of the night by a neighbor who had been sleeping right up until she witnessed the murder. Maybe the woman who died would turn out to be the look-alike and Lora was still alive.

Chapter 4

By the time May rolled around, Georgia and I had emptied out the trunks, and Lonnie had moved them to the basement. The renovations on the attic were underway, and Lonnie was confident that the room would be ready in early June if everything continued to go as smoothly as it had to this point. Georgia and I had decided to organize a series of events beginning the weekend after the grand opening, which we'd scheduled for July 13. We weren't going to begin booking rooms until August, but we were feeling ambitious in anticipation of the early completion of the remodel.

Georgia, Lacy, and I had begun furnishing and outfitting the first three floors of the house. We'd set up the furniture we had and begun putting away kitchenware and linens. We had a list of items we still needed to purchase, but we were finally well on our way.

Trish had stopped by on her way home after visiting her relatives in Lewiston. We'd made copies of letters and journals related to Chamberlain and Abagail Westminster. Most of the letters, journals, and photos we'd found dated from the years the property was run as a resort, but in addition to finding Chamberlain's artwork, we'd found a diary that had belonged to someone named Beatrice and a handful of old photos that I planned to blow up, frame, and hang in the inn. We still hadn't figured out who Emily was, but Trish was going to continue to work on that, and she promised to let us know whatever she found out.

Georgia had spoken to Lonnie about a display for the guest books and other items of historical significance. He was going to build something and in the meantime, Georgia was storing the items she'd identified for the display in the closet in her bedroom. Now that the inn was being outfitted for the grand opening, we seemed to be running out of storage space for items that had not as yet found homes.

"I'm going to spend several hours writing, but I thought we might want to go for a walk along the bluff this afternoon," I suggested after we'd worked together to clean up our small kitchen after breakfast. "It is such a beautiful day and I'm sure Ramos would enjoy a good run."

"Ramos and I would love to come along. I'm going to run over to see Tanner's new puppies this morning, but I'll be back before lunch. I've been wanting to talk to you about the food for the grand opening, so we can talk while we walk."

I picked up a fresh apricot from the bowl. "Okay, it sounds like we have a plan. Tell Tanner hi for me and let him know that I want to come to see the puppies too when I have time."

After Georgia and I had verified our plans, I returned to my bedroom, which I was also using as an office. I tried to focus on my writing, but my mind kept wandering. After several attempts to get into the flow, I logged out of my writing program and logged onto the internet.

The body that had been discovered north of here had been confirmed as the remains of Lora Slavin. Peter Slavin had not been found, but Colt had issued a warrant for his arrest following the verification of his wife's remains. I knew Colt had been turning over rocks, looking for the man, and I had no reason to believe I would stumble upon any information he hadn't already discovered, but I felt antsy and distracted, so decided to do a Google search to see what I could find.

Lora had had a Facebook page. She hadn't been active since before the incident that may have resulted in her death, although her account was still active. According to her bio, she was married to Peter Slavin, lived in Holiday Bay, and was a Maine native. We already knew all that, so I scrolled through her feed. There was a post about the obituary of someone named Wilson Broadmoor, who died in 2014. I began to read it and discovered he was Lora's father. He'd fallen while hiking and broken his neck. He'd been survived by his wife, Irene, and his daughter. No other children were mentioned, leading me to believe the idea of a look-alike sister as Peter's accomplice was probably a dead end. At the time the obituary was written, Lora was referred to as Lora Broadmoor, so she must not have been married yet.

Colt had said that the call about Lora's murder had come in three years ago. Lora's father had died five years ago, so Lora must have married Peter sometime between those events. Her name on her Facebook page was Lora Slavin, though I didn't see a post about the wedding. Odd. Of course, she and I weren't friends, so all I could see were her public posts, so perhaps she'd kept her wedding photos private.

There were several photos of Lora on her page from the early days of her owning the account. It appeared she had friends and participated in a variety of activities, although any photos that would have been posted after she married Peter were hidden from my view. I continued to scroll back in time until I found a series of posts consoling Lora over the death of her grandmother in 2010. I realized if I could find her grandma's obit, I might be able to find out whether she had any cousins. Eventually, I found a link to it. The grandmother's name was Harriet Farmer. From that, I figured she must be the mother of Lora's mother; if she was on Lora's father's side, her last name would likely have been Broadmoor. Her list of "survived by" relatives included her daughters, one of them Lora's mother, the other Hannah Vane, one granddaughter, Lora, and her grandsons, Douglas and Thomas Vane.

It appeared that Lora had only male cousins, at least on her mother's side. I still didn't know who might be lurking around in her father's gene pool.

I wondered if her mother was still alive. I didn't notice any posts relating to her death, but there also weren't any posts older than 2016.

I leaned back in my chair and stared at my computer screen. I looked for information about Irene Broadmoor but came up dry. When I checked for Douglas and Thomas Vane, neither seemed to have Facebook pages. I continued to surf around and finally found a Twitter account for Thomas Vane, a screen and window guy working out of Bangor. Most of his tweets related to his business and the softball team he played on. I didn't find a single tweet that mentioned Lora, but I didn't suppose it was all that odd that he wouldn't mention a cousin he might not even have been close to.

I searched for another fifteen minutes before I stumbled onto a newspaper article about the grand opening of Firehouse Books, a quaint and cozy bookstore in Holiday Bay that was located in what had once been an actual firehouse. The owner was Vanessa Blackstone, and I'd been meaning to introduce myself to her, though I hadn't made time to do it yet. According to the article, Lora Broadmoor was one of the first employees of the store when it opened. Making a quick decision, I logged off my computer, grabbed my keys, and headed out to my SUV.

******

Firehouse Books was in the oldest section of Holiday Bay. The old firehouse had served the town until twelve years earlier when a new facility had been built. The building had stood empty for several years before Vanessa bought, renovated, and opened it as a bookstore in 2013. I loved the ambience of the place from the first minute I walked in the front door.

Not only was it laid out in a way that invited the shopper to sit and read for a spell, but the original fireman's pole was still in the middle of the main floor of the building. It looked like it had been secured from above so no one could actually slide down it, but it was a charming detail to the overall feel of the store.

"Vanessa Blackstone?" I asked the dark-haired woman behind the counter.

"Oh my. You're Abby Sullivan."

I held out a hand. "I am. I imagine Georgia has mentioned that I might stop in at some point."

"She did, and I have been so anxious to meet you. I love your books. My customers love your books. I can't believe you live right here in my hometown."

"I've only lived here for a short time, but I really should have come in sooner. Your store is magical." I looked around at the full bookshelves, colorful walls, and enchanting accent pieces.

"I'd love to do an author signing here when your next book is published."

"I'd be happy to," I responded. "I'll give your name to my publicist so she can make the arrangements. The reason I am here today is to ask about something other than my books, though. Do you have a minute?"

She grinned. "Of course. How can I help you?"

"I understand that Lora Slavin worked for you when you first opened."

Vanessa nodded. "Yes, that is right. She worked for me full time at first, and then part time after she married Peter."

"And how long ago was that?"

The woman placed the first two fingers of her right hand to her jaw and began to tap out her thoughts with her index finger. "I guess Lora and Peter married about four years ago. They were together for a long time before they became engaged and then were engaged for a long time before they married. To be honest, I wasn't sure they would ever make the trip down the aisle, but then Lora's father died and it seemed like Peter, who had always been sort of flighty, took a lot more interest in following through with the commitment they'd made."

"I understand the couple moved a year later."

Vanessa hesitated. "Yes, I guess that is what most folks have been saying."

"Do you think something different occurred?" I wasn't sure who, if anyone, Colt had talked to about Lora's death, so I wanted to tread lightly.

Vanessa hesitated but spoke at last. "There are a few of us who believe that Lora didn't move out of state as we were told by Peter. There are those of us who believe that Lora was killed and Peter only pretended that she had moved ahead of him."

"Erica Kurtzpatrick."

Vanessa nodded. "She could never prove what she said she saw, but I for one believe her. If you knew her, you would believe her as well. Erica is not the sort to make things up or to sensationalize something when she might not have all the facts. If Erica said she saw Peter kill Lora, you can count on the fact that a murder happened."

"I spoke to Chief Wilder, who said that he video-chatted with Lora after Erica claimed to have witnessed Peter killing her."

Vanessa tightened her lips. "I know that he said he saw her, but Peter must have faked the call somehow. I don't know how exactly, but I know Erica would never lie, so that's what must have happened."

"Do you think that the woman Chief Wilder chatted with might have been a look-alike sister, or perhaps a cousin? I know that is one theory Chief Wilder is looking in to."

Vanessa shook her head. "Lora was adopted, so trying to find a sibling or cousin who looked like her would be a waste of time."

Okay, this was news. I wondered if Colt knew about it. He hadn't mentioned it, so I had to assume he didn't.

"Do you know anything about Lora's birth parents?" I asked.

Vanessa shook her head. "No. Lora didn't know anything about them. Apparently, the adoption was a private affair. The files were sealed and the identities of the birth parents weren't revealed to anyone, including the adoptive parents. Lora was never told about the adoption and she assumed for most of her life that her adoptive parents were her birth parents, but she got sick when she was seventeen and needed a kidney, and that was when the truth of her parentage was revealed. According to Lora, even her birth certificate bore the name of her adoptive parents."

"Why all the secrecy?" I wondered.

Vanessa shrugged. "I have no idea. Lora told me that her parents didn't know why there were so many oddities associated with her adoption. Her mom told her that they wanted to have a baby but were unable to, so they chose to adopt. They were having a hard time doing that too until she came along. The attorney they were working said he had a baby in need of placement, but part of the deal was that the adoption would not take place through normal channels. Lora's parents wanted a baby so badly, they agreed to the terms, including a stipulation that they were to tell no one, including Lora, that she was adopted."

"Why would they care if Lora knew she was adopted as long as the identity of the biological parents wasn't revealed?"

"Lora wasn't sure, but her mother told her that the attorney said that the birth parents didn't want Lora to get curious someday and look for them.'

"And after she found out?" I asked.

"At first, Lora's adoptive parents tried to find out who her birth parents were when she became ill, in the hope of finding someone with a kidney for her, but a kidney was found via an anonymous donor and Lora no longer needed a matching organ from a relative and they gave up their search. Lora was curious about her biological parents once she knew she was adopted, but according to what she told me, she didn't spend a lot of time looking for them."

I glanced up as two women walked into the store. They headed to the new books section without asking for help, so I continued. "It sounds as if you knew Lora for a long time."

"We met in high school. After we graduated, we lost touch for a few years, but then one day I ran into her at a local diner and we reconnected. When I got ready to open the bookstore, she asked if I was going to hire anyone to help out. When I said I was, she applied."

Vanessa and I chatted for a while longer until a customer came in who wanted to order a book. I promised to include Firehouse Books in my next book tour and to stay in touch in the meantime. When I left, I headed to Colt's office with the news of Lora's adoption in the event he hadn't discovered that little-known fact on his own.

"What brings you by on this fine spring day?" Colt asked as I walked in through the front door.

"You're in a good mood today."

Colt nodded. "I guess I am. I just found out that the four-week vacation I requested this summer has been approved."

I raised a brow. "Four weeks. Wow. Are you going somewhere?"

"The kids are staying with me while my parents go on a cruise," Colt said, referring to his niece and nephew, who had lived with their grandparents since the death of their parents. "I could have lined up daycare and made it work without the time off, but I really want to spend time with them. I don't plan to go on a long trip while they are with me, but if I am off while they are here, we can spend some time fishing and camping. We might even go on a short road trip. I'm even thinking about taking them to Walt Disney World for a week."

"I'm sure they'd love that. Every kid I have ever met loves Disney."

"I've never been," Colt informed me, "but it must be a lot of fun. And it is the sort of place my parents would never take them, so doing that, and camping, is up to me."

"It sounds like a fantastic idea, but be sure to plan your trip around my grand opening. I really want you to be there. The kids can come as well, if they are here then."

"I will have them the last week and a half in July and the first three weeks in August, so it will be after your grand opening but we will be sure to get together once they do arrive."

"Perfect. I'm really excited to meet them. You talk about them so often that I almost feel as if I know them."

"And they are excited to meet you as well. Especially my nephew, who thinks that being a writer is almost as cool as being a superhero."

I smiled. "I can tell I am going to like this kid."

"We will definitely plan to spend time together when they are here."

I just hoped that spending time with two wonderful kids wasn't going to make me sad and maudlin. I was used to being around Lonnie and Lacy's kids, so perhaps I was past that. "Listen, the reason I stopped in was to ask if you knew that Lora had been adopted."

Colt looked surprised. "I do, but I didn't until recently. How did you find out?"

"Vanessa Blackstone told me. It seems she knew Lora from when they went to high school together."

"I didn't realize you had been investigating Lora's murder."

"I wasn't. At least not until today. I was trying to write but felt blocked, so I did what I always do when I'm blocked and looked for a reason to do anything other than writing. Today, I settled on doing a Google search relating to Lora Slavin and one thing led to another, and eventually, I found Vanessa, who told me that the adoption was very hush-hush. You probably already know this, but Vanessa said that no one, including Lora, knew she'd been adopted until she needed a kidney and her adoptive parents were forced to admit the truth."

"I looked into her adoption but so far I have been unable to find any records relating to Lora's birth or adoption."

"That's odd. Vanessa said that the adoption did not occur through regular channels. There was some sort of deal where the parents weren't even supposed to tell Lora that she was adopted, which is why she didn't find out until she had a medical emergency."

Colt nodded. "That fits my research as well. I've done quite a bit of digging with no luck so far. I figured that knowing who Lora's biological parents are might give me a place to look for someone who came from the same gene pool and could have been persuaded to pretend to be Lora after she was already dead. Normally, even sealed records can be subpoenaed when a murder is involved, but, as I said, so far I've been unable to find a paper trail sealed or otherwise."

"Do you think that's odd?"

Colt nodded. "Very odd."

Chapter 5

The week after my conversation about Lora's adoption with Colt was productive for me. I finally found my writing muse and was cranking out pages at a rate that was impressive even to me. Georgia had been busy as well, dividing her time between playing with Tanner's puppies and working with Lacy to finish furnishing and outfitting the inn. She had a long list of items we still needed to purchase, and I'd promised I would take a day off to go shopping with her within the next week or two.

I knew that Colt was continuing to work on the Lora Slavin murder case. He'd gone back and reinterviewed the neighbors as well as friends of the couple. He still didn't know why Peter might have killed her, or why he would have buried her body so far away, and he had no idea how Peter had managed the fake call after Lora's death, but Colt was assuming he could very well have been the killer, based on the lack of evidence to suggest otherwise.

And Colt was no closer to finding him than he had been when he'd first started looking. His current opinion was that he was either dead himself or had left the country because he had been unable to find anything showing Slavin's presence in the United States farther back than two and a half years ago.

Trish had been in constant touch with Georgia since both had been reading the diaries and letters we'd found in the attic. Trish was planning another visit as soon as her kids were out of school for the summer and she could send them to their grandparents' house again. I imagined that there were lots of other people who were also really invested in their roots, but as I'd told Georgia on several occasions, while I found Trish's research interesting, I couldn't ever picture spending the amount of time and money she had looking for her family history.

"It's a great day to be outside," Georgia said as I stared into space while trying to organize my thoughts. "I thought it might be a good time to go to the nursery to buy flowers for the planter boxes if you are finished writing for the day."

I glanced out the window. It *was* a lovely day. "That sounds like a great idea. Let me just close all this out and we'll go. I need to keep reminding myself that the grand opening will be here before we know it and if we don't keep making progress on our to-do list, we will be in panic mode during the last few weeks."

"I agree." Georgia glanced at the calendar on her phone. "I do think it is important to stay on top of things, but I think we are in good shape. Lonnie and his crew are making good progress on the attic suite, Lacy and I have most of the furniture in place, and the household items we had in storage put away, the landscape architect has the hardscape in as well as most of the trees and large shrubs. This place is really starting to look like an inn."

I logged off my computer and grabbed my purse, and then we headed toward Georgia's truck because it would be better than my SUV to haul the flowers we purchased. "Did you get all the invites we talked about sent off?"

"I did. And the grand opening has been in the newsletter for weeks. I'm not asking for RSVPs, but we have had a lot of people either call, email, or leave a reply on the webpage about how much they are looking forward to the event."

"Despite the fact that it seems that we are in good shape, I will admit that I am beginning to get nervous. We have less than two months left to pull everything together, and while we seem to be keeping up with things, I have this feeling that things are going to get intense as we approach the big day."

Georgia turned and smiled at me. "Don't worry. I have this. I've figured out the menu and created a shopping list, I've rented the extra tables and chairs we'll need as well as the plates and utensils we've discussed. I've ordered the etched wineglasses we plan to give away to our guests. I've had a number of wineries offer to donate wine in exchange for a mention in our newsletter, so we won't need to buy wine. I'll buy the beer and nonalcoholic beverages when I buy the food."

"What about the music and serving staff?"

"I hired Nikki and some of her friends to help serve, and Lonnie and his band are going to provide the music. Trust me, I was a party planner before I became a caterer; I know what to do. I want you to feel free to offer input and ask questions, but I don't want you to worry."

"I'm not worried," I said, even though I was pretty sure we both knew that I had just said that I was.

"I've been thinking about the annuals for the planter boxes," Georgia said, changing the subject. "I think we should decide on a color scheme for this year. We can change the colors up each year if we want to, but deciding on a theme that runs throughout the property might help pull everything together."

"Okay," I agreed. "Did you have something in mind?"

Georgia turned off the highway onto the county road that led to the nursery. "No, I'm open. What colors do you like?"

I thought about it. I liked red and purple, or even yellow and purple or yellow and red. But the event was happening in July, so a patriotic theme might be nice. "How about red, white, and blue?"

Georgia grinned. "I like it. The tablecloths I ordered are white and the dishware is blue, so maybe we can do red napkins. We might want to display a few flags as well."

"And the rocking chairs on the front porch are blue, while the umbrellas for the patio are red. I really do think that red, white, and blue can be our theme."

We continued to discuss the grand opening until we reached the nursery. Luckily, this particular one had a good selection of flowers in all three colors, so we were able to buy a variety of red, white, and blue flowers in differing shapes and sizes. After filling the back of the truck bed with them, we headed back to the estate to commence with the planting. Lonnie and his men had already filled the boxes with soil, so hopefully, the planting could be completed in a couple of days. The planter boxes had been equipped with drip systems, but the flowers would need to be hand-watered until we could get them relocated into their permanent homes.

"So, how are things going with Trish's search for Emily?" I asked as Georgia and I worked side by side to get the flowers replanted.

"She and I weren't able to find anything for the longest time, but just last night Trish found a reference to 'Elizabeth's situation.' The letter Trish found wasn't specific, so there is no way we can know what that referred to. I mean, it really could have been anything, but we both think that she might have had a baby out of wedlock."

"I guess that could explain why Emily was buried in the family plot without a last name. I suppose she might not have taken the father's name, and Elizabeth's parents might not have wanted an illegitimate child to have the Chesterton name."

"While we can't be sure at this point, both Trish and I suspect that Elizabeth might have died either during childbirth or shortly after. So far, we haven't come up with any mention of Emily in the letters or diaries we found, but we suspect that while she might have survived the birth, she didn't live long."

"Based on the sketch by Chamberlain, Emily must have died after he came into the picture. If you remember, his sketch of the graveyard shows Elizabeth's tombstone, but not Emily's."

Georgia sat back on her heels. She brushed her hair from her face with a forearm. "We know that

Abagail and Chamberlain were only married for four months before she died, but we don't know how long they knew each other before that. Chamberlain moved Abagail into this house after they married, but it is huge and must have taken a while to build even if he had a whole crew working on it. I think we should assume that Chamberlain was around for at least a year before they married."

"I guess that is probably true. Still, if Emily was Elizabeth's daughter, I tend to agree that she most likely died at a young age. Although," I added, "just because she was buried near Elizabeth doesn't mean she died at around the same time. She could have lived a long life and still been buried in that same spot if Elizabeth was her mother."

"I guess that is true." Georgia dug her trowel into the dirt. "I suppose we just assumed she'd died shortly after Elizabeth based on the location of her grave, but you're right, the choice of the site may have had more to do with a familial link than the time of death." Georgia paused once again. "Of course, the reality is, we are simply guessing at the fact that 'Elizabeth's situation' referred to a pregnancy. The reference could have been made about anything. Unless we find confirmation of a pregnancy, I suppose it would be best to consider other explanations."

By the time we'd planted all the boxes on the patio we were exhausted, but the outdoor area looked so different than it had before we began. We committed to working on the planter boxes along the walkways the following day. Despite the fact that we had filled up Georgia's truck with flowers, it seemed that we were going to need more.

"Should we pour ourselves a glass of wine and watch the sunset?" I asked.

"That sounds perfect." Georgia looked down at her dirty clothes. "I'm just going to change into a clean pair of shorts first. I feel like I've been rolling in the dirt."

I looked down at my own soiled clothing. "Okay. Let's change and then take wine along with some cheese and crackers out to the gazebo. It has the best view of the water. I can't wait for our first sunset wedding."

"Unless something comes along sooner, our first wedding is in September," Georgia informed me. "The bride-to-be didn't mention whether or not she had a time in mind, but I suppose I can suggest sunset. Of course, it can be cool in the evenings in September, so if they are thinking of an outdoor reception, they might want to have the ceremony earlier in the day."

"Did the group who asked about having a bachelorette party ever confirm?"

"They did, and they will be here at the end of August." Georgia picked up her filthy yard gloves. "I have a feeling once we formally announce we are open, we will have people lining up to stay with us for a special event or couples' vacation."

Chapter 6

It took us a week and two more trips to the nursery to get all the planter boxes filled, but once they were, The Inn at Holiday Bay was transformed into a magical garden by the sea. The landscaper had completed the planting of the lawn and beds, so all we needed to do to have the lush landscape we had envisioned was time and sunshine. Now that the outdoor area was complete, Georgia and I decided to invite our friends for a cookout. We figured we could get everything ready by the following weekend, so Georgia called Tanner, Nikki, and Velma, and I called Lacy and Colt.

"I'm glad you called," Colt said when I got him on the line. "I have news on the Lora Slavin murder. Do you have time for lunch?"

"I do. I'll meet you somewhere so you don't have to come all the way out to the house."

"How about Garcia's at one?"

Garcia's was a Mexican restaurant with outdoor seating right on the water. During the warm months, when you could sit outside on the patio, it was one of my favorite places to eat. "Garcia's at one sounds great. I'll see you there." Garcia's was a fairly casual place for lunch, but I changed out of my ratty shorts and T-shirt in favor of a bright yellow sundress that I knew accentuated the golden tan I'd acquired during the long hours I'd spent in the yard. As soon as I arrived at the restaurant, I was shown to a table along the railing that overlooked the sea where Colt was already waiting. We both ordered the fish tacos and I immediately asked him what he had learned since we had last met.

"I spoke to Lora's friends and neighbors again. The best I can tell, the last time anyone saw Lora in Holiday Bay was on the day of her death."

"So she couldn't have already been out of town, as Peter suggested." I picked up a chip, dipped it in salsa, and nibbled on the tip.

"Exactly. According to Peter, Lora had been away for several days when I called and spoke to him. That much at least was a lie."

"Okay, so let's go over the timeline. When exactly did Peter go to Atlanta for his conference, and when did Erica report seeing the murder taking place across the street at the Slavin home?" I asked.

Colt took a sip of his water and then answered. "According to what I have been able to determine, Peter left for the conference in Atlanta on Sunday; it was to begin on Monday and he was supposed to return home the following Saturday. Erica called in the murder on Wednesday night, which would mean that Peter had been out of town for more than three days by then. According to Peter, Lora had left to visit her friend on Monday, but the woman who lived three doors down from the Slavins' said she saw Lora drive down the street in the Pontiac the couple owned on Tuesday, and a friend saw her in town on Wednesday morning. Now, it is possible that she was delayed and that she had in fact been on her way out of town when she was seen on Wednesday, but because we now know that Lora's remains ended up in a hand-dug grave two hours north of here, I'm thinking that was not the case."

"When you spoke to Lora—or I guess I should say the woman you thought was Lora—were you able to confirm where she was?"

Colt shook his head. "No. The background was neutral. I remember seeing the sky and a tree. I assume that if the call was faked, Peter was in on it. Erica told me at that time that prior to Lora's death, Peter and she had been fighting, and that she even mentioned that she planned to file for divorce. When Erica witnessed the altercation through her window, she shared that initially, she wasn't surprised, given the other late-night shouting matches she'd seen. She wasn't aware that Peter was out of town or that Lora planned to go visit her friend, but she was sure of what she saw."

Our conversation paused as our food was delivered. Once the waiter left, I said what was at the forefront of my mind. "Okay, so Peter must have come back from the conference, killed Lora, wrapped her in a rug, buried her, and then returned."

"That is my best guess at this point. I'm not sure how he got from Atlanta to Holiday Bay and back again because I couldn't find any airline tickets in his name other than the ones he had purchased to and from Atlanta."

"I remember you mentioning during a previous conversation that Erica saw a car in front of the house. Maybe Peter rented a car or even borrowed one, drove back, killed Lora, and then returned."

"It's a long drive between Atlanta and Holiday Bay."

"It is, but it isn't impossible that he could have driven."

"True."

"I wonder why he did it. I suppose that if Erica is to be believed, it sounds like his marriage had become toxic, but why kill her?" I asked. "Why not just divorce her? And why involve at least one other person? The existence of the Lora look-alike you talked to does seem to complicate things."

"I don't disagree, but the concept of Peter and the Lora look-alike working together is all I have."

I took a bite of my taco, pausing to roll an idea around in my mind. "What if there wasn't a Lora look-alike? What if, initially, Lora didn't die? What if there was an event that took place at the Slavin home that night involving Peter and Lora that is what Erica witnessed, but it didn't result in Lora's death? What if she was knocked out or in some way forced to leave with Peter but wasn't actually killed until sometime after that?"

"If I actually did speak to Lora rather than a double, why wouldn't she tell me she was in trouble?" Colt asked.

"Maybe Peter had a gun on her and told her to act naturally."

"Peter was in Atlanta when I called him the following day, so I don't think there was time for Peter to have kidnapped Lora and moved her to another location."

"Okay, so maybe Peter kidnapped Lora and took her to Atlanta. Maybe he threatened to kill her if she didn't act as if everything was fine."

"That is even more complicated than the theory of a double," Colt pointed out. "Besides, it makes no sense at all that Peter would kidnap his own wife and then take her to the conference he was supposed to be attending, and then bring her all the way back to Maine to bury her."

"I suppose my theory really is much too complicated. Is it possible the person Erica saw with Lora on the night she most likely died was someone other than Peter?"

"I don't know," Colt admitted.

I picked up my taco and took a bite, and Colt worked on his meal as well. We were quiet, both trying to work out the situation in our minds. It was a complex mystery, and things might have gone down a couple of different ways. I tried the black beans that came with the tacos. They were surprisingly good. I wasn't usually a fan. As I nibbled on my rice, I tried to figure out whether the fact that Lora was adopted had anything at all to do with whatever had occurred. It seemed like a significant fact, but I couldn't quite decide how it might fit into the scenario.

After Colt and I had finished our meal, he went back to work and I headed home. I really needed to work on my manuscript, but it was such a nice day, I hated to spend it indoors. I could bring my laptop onto the deck and work out there. I'd just pulled into the drive when Lacy called to let me know she might have some news about Emily and would stop by if I was home. She'd tried to call Georgia, but that call had gone to voice mail. I confirmed that I was home and she was welcome to come by. I suspected that Georgia was at Tanner's; she seemed to spend most of her waking hours with our handsome neighbor and his adorable puppies, so I texted her to let her know that Lacy was on her way over with news about Emily if she wanted to join us to hear it.

When Lacy arrived, we sat down at one of the tables Georgia and I had set up on the new patio. I poured us each a glass of iced tea and we settled in for a long chat while Baby Madison napped in her stroller. Lacy would need to leave to pick up the other kids from school in about an hour, but in the meantime, she seemed happy to enjoy the gorgeous view and the company.

"So, what did you find out about Emily?" I asked.

"I have a friend, Connie, whose family has lived in town since the time Chamberlain and Abagail lived in your house. I hadn't chatted with her for quite a while because she just had a baby and I was busy myself, but I ran into her at the Easter parade and we arranged to get together for lunch this week. One thing led to another, and I ended up sharing with her Trish's research and your visit to the Chesterton family graveyard. I also mentioned the mystery of Emily, and Connie offered to look through some old journals she had to see if anyone named Emily was mentioned. She called me this morning to say that her own great-great-grandmother had kept a diary and in it, she talked about Elizabeth and her 'secret.' She didn't specify that the Elizabeth she spoke of was

Elizabeth Chesterton, and she didn't say specifically what the secret might be, but Connie felt that her great-great-grandmother indicated in a roundabout sort of way that Elizabeth was with child even though she wasn't married or even engaged. Connie and I had discussed the idea that Emily could be an illegitimate child when we'd had lunch, and we'd speculated that Emily might have been Elizabeth's child based on where she was buried, so when Connie came across the entry, she decided to dig deeper. Connie found another entry that could be interpreted to read that Elizabeth Chesterton might have died as a result of complications from childbirth. Connie didn't know how believable the diary was, but she had an aunt who had quite a bit of memorabilia from the Chesterton family, and she remembered seeing the name Emily somewhere. I have no idea if any of this will help in the long run, but I thought I'd mention it because you and Georgia seem to have a knack for digging up the information you're looking for."

"I'll let Georgia know, although there are more might-have-beens and could-have-beens than facts in this. Still, it is as good a theory as any, so I'll pass it along. Georgia will be sorry she missed you. I suspect she is over at Tanner's again, playing with the new puppies."

Lacy smiled. "They really are cute. I took the kids to play with them the other day. The older five had a blast. Maddie is still too young and I was afraid to sit her down in the middle of the fray, but she had fun watching her siblings play with the cute baby labs." Lacy looked at her watch. "I should get going. It is so nice and peaceful out here. If I didn't have five children waiting to be picked up, I'd be tempted to take a nap on one of those lounge chairs."

"Feel free to come by and nap here anytime. Oh, and Georgia and I are having a cookout on Saturday; the entire Parker family is invited."

"Sounds like fun. I'll call Georgia to ask her what she wants me to bring." Lacy stood up and looked around. "The landscaping you've done is really fantastic. This place has a whole different feel than it did when you first moved in."

"It is coming together nicely. We are getting excited about the grand opening. Of course, once we start taking in guests, we are going to be a lot busier and our lifestyle is sure to change quite a bit. I have a feeling I will miss the freedom to come and go as I do now. But having guests to meet and get to know will be rewarding as well, and I do have Georgia to take care of most of the day-to-day tasks. I'm really excited to open the door to this next phase of my life."

Chapter 7

The week seemed to fly by and before I knew it, our guests were arriving for the first cookout on our new patio. The sky was blue and the sea calm as a sailboat with colorful sails glided along the surface of the water. Everyone seemed to love our red, white, and blue theme, which we did extend beyond the flowers to the red umbrellas and blue seat cushions Georgia and I had talked about during our drive to the nursery.

"It looks like Rufus has found a comfy place to nap," Lacy said to me, nodding to the oversized, cushioned swing where her twin daughters, Mary and Meghan, were snuggled up with the cat under the canopy, which provided shade and pleasant temperatures.

"They do seem happy," I agreed. "When Rufus first found me, I wasn't sure how he'd do with the chaos that comes with a complete remodel, but he's weathered the noise and multitudes of men coming and going admirably."

"He does seem to be adaptable." Lacy glanced at Georgia, who was sitting on a bench with Nikki. "Seems like Ramos is pretty adaptable as well." The dog was lying near Georgia and Nikki, who were playing quietly with one of the puppies Tanner had brought along on the outing. One of the most important elements to early training was socialization in a variety of situations, so when Tanner had puppies, he usually had one in tow, no matter what he might be doing.

"What do you know about Nikki's guy?" I asked Lacy, after glancing at the grilling area, where Colt and Lonnie were chatting with Tanner and Jack.

Lacy glanced at the group. "I like him all right. He seems nice enough. I understand that Nikki and Jack have moved their relationship to the next level and are now officially girlfriend and boyfriend. I know it is none of my business, but in my opinion, Jack is much too old for Nikki. I'm sort of surprised that Tanner is letting them see each other. Nikki is mature for her age, and I get that she might be attracted to an older man, but a twenty-year-old woman dating a forty-year-old man seems a bit much."

"I agree, although I'm not sure Tanner has much of a say in who Nikki dates. He is her brother, not her father. Nikki is pretty strong-willed, and she *is* an adult. I don't see her taking advice from her brother even if he offered it." I glanced at the man again. "And I also agree that, on the surface, Jack seems like a nice enough guy, but there is something about him that sort of creeps me out. I can't put my finger on it exactly, but when I met him, I just had this feeling that he was not one to be trusted."

Lacy glanced back toward Nikki. "I know what you are saying. Jack does have this way of looking at you that feels sort of invasive. Nikki is young and still trying to find her way. Her relationships in the past haven't lasted all that long. Maybe this one won't either."

I hoped so. I really didn't want to see Nikki hurt, and I had a feeling this guy would end up hurting her. I glanced toward the back door of the house. "Speaking of relationships that have survived over time…" I said as Velma walked out onto the patio. "Did you notice that she was with Royce at the parade?"

"I did notice and she introduced us," Lacy confirmed. "I was so curious about him after you told me that you'd run into him on Nantucket. He seems like a really nice guy and Velma seems smitten, although she would never admit it. I hope he comes around more often. I think that there is still a spark between them, even though Velma has assured us he is only a friend."

"I invited him to the grand opening and he assured me he would be here, so if he doesn't come around before that, we should see him then." I waved to Velma, who waved back and started in our direction.

"I love what you've done with the place," she said after hugging me hello.

"I like the way it turned out," I answered. "Georgia and I worked around the clock for several days to get all these flowers planted, but we feel it was worth it and are both happy with the way it brightens up the place."

"I couldn't agree more. The splash of color presented by the red umbrellas really pulls you in the minute you walk out onto the patio, and I love the flowers you selected. When you started this project, I knew you had a long road ahead, but everything has come together so very nicely. I'm really excited about your grand opening. You and Georgia should be proud of what you've created."

"We are, although we couldn't have done it without Lacy and Lonnie," I added.

"Of course," Velma agreed.

"It was nice seeing Royce at the parade," I segued into the topic I really wanted to discuss.

"Yes, his showing up the way he did was quite a surprise."

"I hope you had a nice visit," I added. "I really like him. He has an energy I enjoy."

"He is quite the character. And yes, we did have a nice visit. I didn't think I wanted to take the walk down memory lane that he insisted on, but once we got started, I found I rather enjoyed taking a step back in time and reliving some of the highlights."

"Is he planning another visit in the near future?" I asked. "I'd love for us all to go to dinner so I can get to know him a bit better."

Velma frowned. "I'm not sure when or even if he might be back. We didn't make any plans for the future." She sighed. "We had a nice time together, but that might have been the end of it. Royce is a busy man with a life away from here. I enjoy spending time with him, but we never seemed to get our lives lined up when it came to location in the past. Things are no different now."

I supposed that Velma had a point, although Royce had said he would be here for the grand opening. I supposed he might not have mentioned that to Velma yet.

She wandered away to chat with Georgia and Nikki, and Lacy went to check on her three rambunctious boys, so I went inside to check on the side dishes Georgia had left warming in the oven. The baked beans looked and smelled delicious, and Georgia made the best potato salad I'd ever tasted. The guys were grilling the steaks and chicken, the green salad was done and only needed to be tossed with dressing, and the bread was buttered and waiting to be heated.

Colt wandered inside. "Do you need any help?"

"No. It looks like Georgia has everything handled. I knew she would, but I felt I should check on things anyway."

"The place looks great. And finished."

"It almost is," I confirmed. "Lonnie and his men are just finishing up in the attic and then we will be ready for business."

"Are you planning to open early?" Colt asked.

"The grand opening is in July. We are taking reservations beginning in August."

"And after that?"

"We have a few openings in September, but our murder mystery Halloween event, which we have planned for October, has all the weekends booked."

Chapter 8

"Oh my God, oh my God, oh my God," I screamed as I ran out of my bedroom and hugged Georgia as tightly as I could.

"What is it?" Georgia responded with a tone of panic.

"It's Annie." I pulled back and then hugged Georgia again.

"Is she okay?" Georgia looked confused and Ramos had started barking at my crazy behavior.

I took a deep breath and took a step back. I wiped a tear from my cheek. "Annie is fine. I just got an email from her. She is coming to the grand opening."

Georgia's lips grew into a grin. "She's coming?"

I nodded. Georgia hugged me tightly once more and we both started jumping up and down, which really got Ramos howling.

"She asked if we will have a room that she and my brother-in-law can use. She said they plan to stay overnight and then head out the next morning.

Apparently, they are doing a tour of New England and included us as one stop on the way. We planned to have the inn open to view, so there will be people going in and out of the rooms all day, but it sounded like they won't be arriving in Holiday Bay until the day of the open house itself, so once the daylong event comes to a close, the rooms will be empty and they can have their choice."

"I think that is a very workable plan," Georgia said. "Maybe we can even convince them to stay longer."

I hugged my arms to my chest. "Maybe, but even one night feels like such a victory. I'm so happy right now, I feel like I might burst."

Georgia hugged me once again. I knew that she was almost as happy about the fact that Annie was coming for a visit as I was. Georgia had a huge capacity for empathy and I knew that she'd shared my pain; now that things were turning around, she shared my joy.

"What are your plans for the day?" I asked her once I'd settled down a bit. It was already June and the grand opening was coming up quickly.

"Lacy is coming over later to help me finish outfitting the bathrooms and arranging the furniture in the suites. She has a list of items we still need. We talked about another shopping trip later in the week, if you can fit it in. I know you need to finish your manuscript by the end of the month."

"I can fit it in. Really, any day is good. Just let me know when it works for Lacy."

"I'll check with her. I'm going to head over to the basement this morning to look around for anything else that may have been stored in the attic since the

Westminster era. Trish is still working on her family tree and hopes to fill in some of the blanks relating to Emily."

"I thought we all but decided that Emily was Elizabeth's illegitimate child."

"Well, it does seem as if Elizabeth might have died during childbirth, although we have no proof of that. Even if that is true and Elizabeth did have a child out of wedlock, we don't know for certain that Emily was that child, and even if she was, we don't know whether she died shortly after or if she went on to live a long life. The sketch of the cemetery that we found in the attic showed Elizabeth's grave but not Emily's, so we've been assuming that Emily lived for at least a period of time after Elizabeth. As of the time the sketch was drawn, Abagail's grave marker did not appear, so we are assuming she was still alive. That gives us something of a timeline, but without more information, I don't see how we can know for certain who Emily was or how or when she died." Georgia got up and put her coffee cup in the dishwasher. "Anyway, I told Trish I'd head over to give the stuff we haven't sorted through yet a better look this morning. If Lacy shows up before I get back, let her know where I am."

"I will, and let me know if you find anything interesting."

After Georgia left, I took a walk through the garden. Rufus and Ramos both came along, so it was the three of us who set out to enjoy the beautiful summer day. The work on the landscaping was finished. The hardscape was in, the shrubs, trees, and flowers had been planted, and the lawn, which had been laid out in rolls of sod, was beginning to turn a lush green thanks to an automatic irrigation system. The estate was really beginning to feel like a home. A wonderful, beautiful, seaside home. The secret paths that we had included once the shrubs and trees grew to their full height were now open paths that meandered among teeny, tiny shrubs and trees, but the seeds of the garden of our dreams had been planted, and with plenty of sun and some time to grow, I knew that in a few years the garden we'd envisioned would become a reality.

There were a few workmen around this morning, but that predictable sight would soon be coming to an end. Lonnie and his men were just finishing the attic and would be wrapping things up within the next week or two. Georgia and Lacy were still working on furnishing and outfitting, but other than taking care of a few last-minute details, I felt like we were ready for our opening. Not that we would open early even if we could. The grand opening ceremony on July 13 was to be our launch event. We would be easing into our schedule, and when August rolled around, we were booked to capacity clear through mid-September. We had a wedding at the end of September and then we'd segue right into the haunted weekend events that we'd planned for the month of October.

After Rufus, Ramos, and I returned from our walk, I decided to get in a couple of hours of writing time. I had just finished a chapter when Georgia came running in through the front door.

"Abby," she called.

"In here," I yelled.

She opened the door to my bedroom. "I came across a box of things left behind by Bodine Devine and I think I found something important."

"About Emily?" I asked.

"Actually, no. I think what I found might help Colt with the mystery of Lora Slavin."

Georgia handed me a newspaper dated June 2013, which was the year that Devine purchased the estate from Lester Folkman. On the Community News page was an article about his plans for the estate, plans that I knew would never see the light of day. I glanced at Georgia. "This story is interesting, I suppose, but how will this help Colt?"

"Look at the story below it."

The story on the bottom half of the page was about the opening of Firehouse Books. "I found this online," I informed Georgia.

"Yes, I recognized it as such, but the story online didn't have the photo attached. Check it out."

At the bottom of the page, below the article, was a photo of the store's owner, Vanessa Blackstone, and her employee, Lora Broadmoor. At first, I didn't see what Georgia was so excited about, but then I looked at the crowd that had gathered around the old firehouse for the ribbon cutting and noticed that a woman who looked exactly like Lora was standing among the spectators. "Other than the fact that this woman has longer hair, she looks just like Lora," I said.

"Exactly. You and Colt have been kicking around the theory that it might have been a Lora look-alike that Colt spoke to. You told me that since the beginning, he was settled on the idea that Lora might have been abducted and killed later, which sort of fits, but that theory doesn't explain why she would be wearing a pink nightgown when she was buried, or why she would be rolled in the rug that came from the

Slavins' dining-room floor, but if Lora actually did have a double…"

"Then maybe she did die at the house on the night Erica saw her being attacked and maybe it was this double Colt spoke to." I looked at the photo again. "I wonder who she is. I wonder if Lora knew her. I wonder if she was at the grand opening of the bookstore intentionally or if she just stumbled upon it and found not only a new bookstore but her exact double."

"It does seem that even if Lora hadn't seen the woman in the crowd, the woman would have seen her," Georgia agreed.

I looked at the photo one more time. "What exactly are we saying?"

Georgia narrowed her gaze. "I'm not sure. I think you should call Colt. If Lora had an exact double—and this photo seems to indicate that she did—the assumptions that can be made about what might have occurred on the night she died would be quite different from the ones you can assume if Lora was alive to speak to Colt on that video chat."

I called Colt, who agreed to come right over. Just from what he heard on the phone, he thought that if Lora did have a double, that would open up additional possibilities.

******

Colt, Georgia, and I took chairs on the small deck off the back of the cottage with tall glasses of iced tea before us. I jumped in with the thoughts that had been running through my mind since Georgia found the photo, and addressed my comment to Colt. "We know that Lora was adopted, but so far you have been unable to find her adoption records. As far as we know, she died without ever knowing who her biological parents were, but given the fact that there are two women with Lora's face in this photo, I think we can entertain the possibility of Lora having a twin sister."

"Following so far," Colt said.

"So, what if this twin, who we should assume was most likely also put up for adoption, just happened to attend a grand opening event and came upon a woman who looked exactly like her."

"Still following, but how does this lead to Lora being murdered three years later?" Colt asked.

I frowned. "I'm not sure, but perhaps after the twin happened across Lora at the bookstore opening she became curious. Maybe that caused her to dig into her own past. Maybe whatever she found created a situation in which she felt it advantageous to have Lora dead."

"Advantageous how?" Colt asked.

I shrugged. "I don't know. I'm just spitballing, but maybe the biological parents of the twins were wealthy and planned to leave their fortune to the twin girls they had birthed but had not raised. Maybe Lora's twin found that out and decided to kill her so that she could receive the entire inheritance."

Colt chuckled. "Sounds like a good plot for one of your books, but I don't think that theory will stand up under the light of day."

"Why not?"

Colt took a sip of his tea. "It is too complicated. If Lora's biological parents were wealthy, why would they have put their daughters up for adoption in the first place? Why not hire a nanny to raise them if they weren't interested in doing it themselves? Even if they felt that putting them up for adoption was in their best interest, why separate them? There are plenty of couples looking for babies who would have taken both of them. And even if they did decide to give them away and separate them for some reason, why would they seek out a nontraditional adoption which did not appear to have left a paper trail? And even if we could explain all of that, why turn around and leave their fortune to them? And even if all of that were true, how would Lora's twin discover all of it given the fact that the adoption records don't seem to be readily available, and then kill her sister just so that she could collect double?"

"Okay, so the theory is complicated, but it isn't impossible," I said.

"No, it isn't impossible," Colt admitted. "Completely unlikely, but not impossible."

"It seems to me that the next best move might be to find the missing link," Georgia said. "If you consider that perhaps Peter did not kill Lora, who did? The killer was a male with features similar to Peter. If you find the real murderer, maybe he will have the rest of the story."

"Unless it actually was Peter who killed Lora," I said. "I know we are batting around the theory of a killer other than Peter right now, but we don't know that Peter didn't come home and kill his wife and then team up with her double to provide an alibi. It is possible and it is the simplest theory."

"I don't disagree," Colt responded, "but if the motive for murder did have something to do with the fact that Lora had a twin, it would be easier to find the twin if one exists, than to figure out who the killer was. I'll do a search to see what I can come up with."

"You might want to look for someone who lives or lived in the little town near where they found Lora's body," I suggested. "There must be a reason why it was buried all the way up there."

Colt finished off his tea. "I'll start there." He turned to Georgia. "And thanks for the new lead. Admittedly, it is a confusing lead right now, but in the end, I think it will help us get the case closed."

"I hope that if Lora did have a twin, that she wasn't the one who killed her," Georgia said. "The whole thing will seem so much worse if it turns out that is what happened."

"Either Lora or someone who looked like her spoke to me after Erica witnessed the murder that night. The person I spoke to used a phone that was connected to the number Peter gave me, which indicated proximity to Lora," Colt reminded her. "Either Lora was still alive at that point and was the person I spoke to, or her double was involved and lied to make me believe Lora was still alive. If this double was involved, you can bet she was most likely working with the killer."

The idea that Lora might have been killed by her own sister, even if it was a sister she had never met, suddenly made this case much more depressing.

Chapter 9

As the days of June faded and the hot summer descended upon us, Georgia and I grew both excited and nervous for the grand opening and the realization of a dream we had been working toward since the previous November. The renovations were completed, the remainder of the furniture, linens, and kitchenware purchased, and the landscape perfected. Georgia had been working to stock nonperishable food items in the pantry. We, of course, would shop for the perishable items we'd need for the grand opening a day or two beforehand.

Trish still hadn't found any conclusive evidence of the identity of Emily, but she had accepted our invitation to attend the grand opening and was arriving a day early to pick the brains of any locals who had lived in town for several generations. Quite a few families had lived in Holiday Bay and the surrounding area for three or more generations. I found the continuity heartwarming. To live in the same house as your grandparents had might not be everyone's cup of tea, but I for one was enamored with the idea of passing a single plot of land down from one generation to the next.

Velma had confirmed with us that Royce would be attending the grand opening after all. I'd planned to offer him a room at the inn, but as it turned out, he would be staying with Velma. I wasn't sure what to make of that exactly. Velma did have a three-bedroom house, so the fact that he was staying with her didn't necessarily mean they had renewed their romance, but maybe…

Annie had emailed again to confirm that she and Arnie would be arriving on the day of the grand opening and spending one night at the inn. I'd emailed back to say how much I was looking forward to seeing both of them. After they arrived, I hoped to convince them to stay longer, but even twenty-four hours with my sister was more than I had hoped for until a few weeks ago; however long her visit was, I was thrilled.

Georgia had hired Nikki and a few of her friends to help out at the event. Tanner would be coming, and I was sure that Georgia would hook him into helping as well. Colt was still working on the Lora Slavin case, which he hoped to have wrapped up before his niece and nephew arrived and he started his four-week vacation, but he'd offered to help out if need be, and the way things usually went, I was sure we'd need all the help we could get.

"Did you order the flowers for the tables?" I asked Georgia after she and Ramos returned from walking down to the end of the drive to pick up the mail.

"I did. They will be delivered on the Friday before the opening. I have the tables, chairs, linens, and dishware that we ordered arriving on Thursday, giving us plenty of time to set everything up. I've ordered business cards, flyers, pamphlets, and the souvenir wineglasses to hand out, and I even ordered toiletries for the bathrooms with our logo on them."

"It sounds like you are on top of this."

Georgia sorted the mail as she spoke, tossing each envelope on the kitchen counter as she went. "I am. As I said before, I don't want you to worry. I've ordered the wine and seafood, I have a huge order in with the local farmers market, and I have fresh eggs and dairy products coming from nearby farms and dairies. I'd like the food we serve to be organic and local as much as possible, so I have been making the rounds, meeting folks, and establishing networks. Everything is going to be perfect. I promise."

I hoped Georgia was right, but I couldn't quite quell the knot in my stomach.

Georgia handed me a large envelope. "This is for you. It's from San Francisco."

I took the envelope and opened it. It was an official letter from the SFPD Internal Affairs department, letting me know that some of Ben's cases had been reviewed and that the process was complete, with all questions about his conduct answered and cleared. In a way, I found it odd that I was receiving this letter now after not hearing a peep when the investigation was initiated, but I supposed I should just be relieved that I had formal confirmation of the fact that the investigation had been concluded and no evidence of wrongdoing had been found.

I thought about calling Colt to let him know that I had received the letter, but I had a long to-do list today, so I decided it could wait until I saw him. I tossed the letter on the counter and headed into my bedroom to dress for the day. Georgia wanted me to attend a Holiday Bay business owner's meeting with her so that I could meet the individuals whose referrals we would need to grow our business, and I had agreed to be there despite my resistance to do so up to this point. In the past, I'd maintained that we had plenty of time to establish these relationships, but now that plenty of time had dwindled down to a couple of weeks, so if there was ever going to be a good time to commit, it was now.

******

The Holiday Bay Business Owners Association met on the first Monday of every month. Today, July 1, was one such Monday, and a monthly meeting was being held despite the fact that almost everyone was busy with preparations for the Fourth of July weekend. The Fourth was on a Thursday this year, so the traveling carnival was set to arrive tomorrow, the parade was scheduled for Thursday morning, and the fireworks show would commence after dark on Thursday evening. There was also a community softball tournament, a pancake breakfast, and bands and crafts in the park over the weekend. In addition, pretty much every mom-and-pop shop on the main streets of the small town had sales and special offers going on all week.

"The local animal shelter is holding a pet adoption clinic on Saturday," one of the women whose name I had not yet learned informed the group. "They wanted to use the bandstand, but the bands we have scheduled for the afternoon need to use it. I suggested to the animal shelter folks that they use the grassy area at the foot of the bandstand, but they were afraid that having the bands playing so close to the animals would have an adverse effect on them. Then I asked the shelter folks if they would be willing to move over to the high school parking lot, but they pointed out that the park was the happening place to be, and they really wanted the increased exposure the bandstand area would provide."

"Who was scheduled first?" a woman wearing a smart business suit asked.

"The pet adoption folks applied to use the bandstand months ago. The events committee didn't schedule the bands and other events to be held in the park until well after. I suppose if the decision comes down to first come, first served, we will need to move the bands and allow the pet adoption folks to use the park. If we decide that an event to bring in tourists and promote the community is more important, though, I'm sure we can find a way to force the pet adoption folks to move over to the high school."

Personally, I felt like the pet adoption should be held in the park because they had reserved the area well ahead of the event committee, but being new to the group I decided to listen rather than offer an opinion. At least for now.

"We've been featuring bands in the park over the Fourth of July weekend for years," one of the men offered. "The committee might not have officially applied for the permit until after the pet adoption folks did, but there should be some sort of grandfathering in at work here. The animal shelter folks must have known that the park was going to be utilized for family events that particular weekend."

"I'm sure they did," the moderator answered. "Which is probably why they wanted to hold their clinic that particular weekend."

"Is the only event affected by the pet adoption clinic the bands?" asked a woman I recognized as owning a bakery.

"It is," the moderator confirmed. "The animal shelter only wants to use the bandstand for part of the day, so the softball game, food court, and community picnic would not be affected."

"Can the bands be moved to the other end of the park near the playground?" someone asked.

"No electrical," someone else said.

"Maybe the bands can just start later," I eventually spoke up. "After the adoption clinic is over for the day."

"Currently, the pet adoption clinic is set to run until two o'clock and the bands are set to begin at noon, so there is only a two-hour window where the events conflict," someone else said.

"Yeah, but the shelter folks will need to clean up and move the animals who were not adopted, and the band will need to set up, so I think we'd need to push the first band back to three o'clock, which would cause all the bands to be pushed back. The bands are supposed to wrap up at eight. If we push them back three hours, they won't wrap up until eleven, which is much too late." It was the man who had spoken before who explained all this.

This discussion went on for a good thirty minutes until the group finally decided to speak to the pet adoption folks about turning their one-day event into a two-day one running in the mornings only so that it wouldn't interfere with the bands at all. I wasn't sure they'd go for it, but I supposed it was worth a try.

Once that was decided, the group discussed the parade and the problems they were having with the designated route, and then a fifteen-minute break was called. Georgia entered into a conversation with the woman who owned the flower shop, so I headed to the table where a coffeepot had been set up.

"You're Abby Sullivan," a woman with dark blond hair said to me as I added a dollop of cream to my cup.

"I am. And you are?"

"Tessa Sanders. I recognized you from the photo on the jacket of your books. I'd heard you'd moved to Holiday Bay and have been hoping to run into you. I love your books."

I smiled. "Thank you. I'm happy to meet you. I assume you are a business owner?"

"Veterinarian. I don't always come to these meetings, but the woman who runs the animal shelter had an emergency and couldn't make it, so I agreed to pop in and make sure they didn't move the adoption clinic to some random place where we wouldn't get any exposure."

"Do you think changing the hours the clinic runs so that it won't interfere with the bands will work?"

Tessa shrugged. "It isn't up to me, but the folks at the shelter are community-minded, so I think it might. I'm going to suggest they try to have a presence on the Fourth as well if they can find volunteers to handle it."

"I'd be happy to help out," I offered. "If what you need are bodies, that is. I'm certainly not an expert on animals—far from it, in fact—but I can chat with people and help them fill out paperwork."

Tessa smiled. "Thank you. Having someone with your name recognition would be huge. I'll have the organizer call you to arrange for a time for you to help."

I pulled out one of my Inn at Holiday Bay business cards and jotted down my cell number on the back. "Have her call me at this number."

Tessa accepted the card. "The Inn at Holiday Bay. You must be working with Georgia."

"You know Georgia?"

Tessa nodded. "She brought Ramos in for shots and we got to chatting. She told me all about the inn. It sounds wonderful."

"You should come to the grand opening. It will start at two o'clock on July 13 and run until everyone leaves. Georgia has a ton of food planned and it will be a good opportunity for anyone who is interested to take a tour."

"I'll make a point to drop in. I've been inside that house before, you know."

"Have you? When was that?"

"When I was a kid. I guess I was around nine or ten, so that must have been around 1990. A man named Lester Folkman owned the house and property at that time, although he didn't live in the area, so the house was empty."

"So how did you manage to get inside?" I asked.

"My family has lived in this town for five generations, so we have a lot of connections. My dad knew that Mr. Folkman wanted to sell, and while my dad had nowhere near the financial means to buy it, he managed to talk the Realtor into letting him inside to check things out. Dad let me come along when he took the tour. I remember the place was stale and dusty, and all the furniture was covered with sheets. The electricity was off, of course, so the lighting was dim, and I was sure the house must be haunted. Not that I saw any ghosts, but the house was old and tended to be creaky, and it seemed to be extra-creaky that day."

"If your family has been here for that long, you must have ancestors who knew Chamberlain and Abagail Westminster."

Tessa nodded. "My great-grandmother dated George Gram for a while. George was Abagail's nephew. He eventually married someone else, but she and George remained friends. She used to talk about him all the time. It seems that for her, he was the one who got away."

"If I remember correctly, George was the eldest son of Celeste Chesterton, Abagail's younger sister."

"Yes. That is correct."

"I recently met Maria Gram's great-granddaughter. Her name is Trish and she is working on her family history."

Tessa raised a brow. "Really? How fascinating. Does she live here?"

"No, but she will be here next week. If you want to leave me your cell number, I will arrange for you to meet her."

"I'd love that." Tessa gave me one of her business cards. "My cell is on the bottom under my business line."

"Great. I'll call you when Trish gets into town. In the meantime, please do have the pet adoption clinic organizer call me about helping out."

By the time Tessa and I were wrapping things up, the meeting was being called back to order. Tessa slipped out the side door after whispering that she needed to get back to work, and I sat down next to Georgia again. I found myself wishing that I too could slip out the side door, but I supposed that Georgia was correct that if we were going to have a local business, we needed to be involved in the community and the events that were held to bring in the tourist dollar.

"I see you met Tessa," Georgia whispered to me.

I nodded. "I did. She is very nice. I even found myself volunteering to help out with the adoption clinic."

"That's great. I'm doing it as well. Maybe we can work the same shift. I'll try to arrange it."

"That would be great. Did you know that Tessa's family has lived in Holiday Bay for generations? Her great-grandmother dated George Gram."

Georgia raised a brow. "Really? I wonder if she knows who Emily was."

"I didn't think to ask her, but we should. Maybe she can fill in all the blanks for Trish."

After the meeting, Georgia and I went over to Velma's for lunch. It would be a late lunch because the meeting had run long, but a late lunch could also be considered an early dinner. I hadn't really wanted to go to the meeting, but now I was glad I had. In addition to meeting Tessa, who I felt a real connection with, Georgia had introduced me to at least a dozen other people.

When we arrived, Velma was just getting ready to close for the day, but she invited us in and was fine with making us anything we wanted. We both chose Cobb salads and glasses of iced tea. Velma made three salads, deciding to join us before helping her staff with the chores of cleaning up, and we settled in one of the booths at the back of the café.

"So, how was the meeting?" Velma asked Georgia.

Georgia filled her in. During the winter, Velma was closed on Mondays and so was able to attend the meetings herself, but during the summer she was open seven days a week with the help of summer staff who hired on with her every summer.

"And did you enjoy the meeting?" Velma asked me, knowing it was my first one.

"To be honest, I'm not really the sort to like those sort of things, but I met the local veterinarian, and we seemed to hit it off."

"Tessa is great." Velma nodded. "I should have thought to introduce you sooner."

"Abby even volunteered to help out at the pet adoption clinic," Georgia said.

Velma chuckled. "Are you sure you're the same person who told me that you weren't a cat person or really any kind of pet person when I first met you just over six months ago?"

I smiled. "I will admit that I didn't think I was a pet person, but Rufus changed my mind. Now I can't imagine life without him, and Ramos...well, Ramos is just a huge ball of love. Talk about a sweetie."

"Did you happen to meet Gloria Driscoll?" Velma asked.

I shook my head. "No, that name doesn't ring a bell."

"She wasn't there today," Georgia added.

"That's too bad. Gloria is a good connection to have. She has lived here her entire life and knows everyone. She works down at the harbor during the summer months. Her family owns the marina. In fact, I think her great-great-grandfather built it. Anyway, if you get the chance, you should introduce yourself. A lot of the tourists who come into town ask her for food and lodging recommendations."

"Do you think she might know anything about Chamberlain Westminster or the Chesterton family, considering her family has lived in town that long?" I asked.

Velma shrugged. "She might. It can't hurt to ask. I can think of four or five families who have been around that long too if you are really interested."

I asked Velma for the list and figured that we could follow up with them when Trish got here.

"I chatted with Colt when he was in for lunch today," Velma said, changing the subject. "Sounds like he has a lead on Lora Slavin's look-alike."

"Does he?" I asked. "I haven't spoken to him since Saturday."

"He was finally able to trace Lora's history back to her birth. As it turns out, she wasn't put up for adoption by her biological parents after all; she was kidnapped when she an infant and never seen by her parents again."

Wow. I hadn't seen that coming. "Kidnapped?"

Velma nodded. "It turns out that she was a California Brookvale. Her mother, Olivia Brookvale, delivered twin daughters, Scarlett and Sophia. When she was just three months old, Sophia disappeared from her nursery. It was long suspected that one of the household staff snuck her out, but they could never prove it. A massive search for Sophia was conducted, but the investigators didn't find a single clue to explain what had happened to her. The Brookvales were a very wealthy family, so it was assumed they'd receive a ransom demand, but they never did. The twins would have been thirty-seven this fall."

"Are you saying that the couple who raised Lora—or Sophia, I guess—kidnapped her?"

Velma shook her head. "Colt said that Lora's adoption was private, and at this point, they don't suspect her parents of any wrongdoing. When Lora was adopted, it was made clear to them that all information about the birth parents and the baby's history was to be sealed, but Colt didn't believe that the couple suspected that the baby had been kidnapped. I understand Lora didn't even know she had been adopted until the problem with her kidney. When the identity of the birth parents still was not revealed despite the life-and-death situation, everyone pretty much assumed it never would be."

"So even if Lora didn't know who her biological parents were or that she had a twin, if she had been kidnapped, both her biological parents and perhaps even her twin sister would have known about the second daughter, even if they didn't know who or where she was."

"That's what Colt thinks," Velma confirmed.

"So when Scarlett ran into Lora at the opening of the bookstore, she must have realized who she was," Georgia said.

"That is Colt's belief as well. At this point, he is assuming that Scarlett recognized Lora as being Sophia but didn't approach her for some reason. She may have been unsure of what to do and wanted to speak with someone else before acting, or she may have felt threatened by Lora and decided to hide what she'd discovered. He suspects, though, that it was Scarlett he spoke to after Lora was murdered, so in his mind, she is involved no matter what is going on."

"Has he been able to track her down?" I asked.

"Not yet. But he is working on it, so you might want to touch base with him when you get a chance."

"I will."

The three of us discussed the new development a while longer but couldn't decide whether Scarlett was the mastermind and had hired someone to kill her long-lost sister or if Peter was involved in some way. The only reason I could come up with for Scarlett to kill her sister was money, but the idea that one twin would kill the other over a few bucks, even if it was a few million bucks, was too depressing to consider.

Chapter 10

When Georgia and I returned home, I called Colt to ask about the investigation. It sounded like he had made a lot of progress since the last time I'd seen him. He answered my call but said he was in the middle of an important call and asked if we could meet for dinner. I suggested takeout at the beach, which he thought was a wonderful idea, and offered to pick me up when he got off work for the day. I hung up and went in search of Georgia, who'd gone outside with Ramos when we first arrived home. The estate seemed so quiet now that Lonnie and his crew had finished their work and were no longer around. I knew that once we began having guests our peace and quiet would be a thing of the past, so I decided to embrace the serenity and enjoy it while I could.

"I called Trish to confirm that she will be here on Friday of next week," Georgia shared after I'd joined her in the garden. Ramos was lounging with Rufus on the grass under a shady tree.

"It's going to be a busy week. In fact, this week will be busy as well. We will need to stay organized."

"We *are* organized and everything is going to go perfectly," Georgia assured me for at least the millionth time. "Other than making the food, we are ready for the grand opening. And as for the events in town this week, we'll participate to the extent we have the time and energy to do so and pass on the rest."

I sat down on a bench near where Georgia was weeding. "You're right. I am way overthinking things. The parade will be fun and we don't have a float in this one to worry about. The fireworks should be entertaining, and again, we aren't expected to participate in any way. Beyond that, we will just play it by ear."

"Exactly. Did you get hold of Colt?"

"He was busy, so we are going to get together this evening. It sounded, based on what Velma shared, that he has made a lot of headway in the past couple of days."

Georgia sat back on her heels. "Colt is a smart guy. He'll figure this out."

"I hope so. It is a complicated case." I knelt down and began helping Georgia. "In some ways, none of it makes sense."

"Maybe it doesn't make sense because we don't have all the pieces yet," Georgia said.

"Maybe. We are heading to the beach for a picnic if you want to come."

"Thanks, but I've made plans with Tanner."

I glanced at Georgia. "Date plans?"

She shrugged. "I suppose that there are those who would view sailing as a date, but I prefer to think of it as an activity I am sharing with a friend."

I glanced up toward the sky. "It seems like the perfect day to go sailing."

Georgia nodded. "We are going to do a sunset cruise, but I agree, it is a perfect day. Just enough of a breeze to encourage the boat along, but not so much as to make it choppy. It is warm, but not hot. I am really looking forward to it."

There were times I wondered when Tanner and Georgia would move their relationship along, but Georgia didn't seem ready to make that move and Tanner seemed content with waiting. Still, from what I knew of both my friends, I had a feeling the transition from friend to more than that couldn't be much longer in coming.

******

Colt surprised me with a basket filled with creative selections that he'd had his receptionist, Peach, put together. Normally, I would question the appropriateness of asking the woman who had been hired to answer phones and file paperwork to put the basket together, but I knew Peach well enough to be sure that she was likely thrilled to have been asked to tackle the task. In fact, knowing Peach, Colt probably mentioned takeout and she was the one to come up with the entire picnic idea.

The beach was crowded, as it was every day in the summer, but we managed to find a table with both a view and some shade. Colt set out the plates and containers with the food while I opened the wine and poured two glasses.

"This is really nice," I said.

"It is. I'm glad it worked out. I live in this beautiful community with some of the most beautiful beaches anywhere and most of the time I am so busy that I neglect to even notice."

"I'm sure you'll make up for lost time when the kids are here. They'll probably want to have dinner at the beach every day."

Colt took a sip of his wine. "I'm sure they will. And I am really excited about their visit. I just hope I can get this murder wrapped up before they arrive."

"When I spoke to Velma, it sounded like you'd made progress."

Nibbling on a piece of cheese, Colt agreed that he had. He explained pretty much everything Velma had already told Georgia and me and added that it was his idea to research kidnapping cases, given the secrecy of Lora's adoption, which led him to the Brookvale kidnapping in the first place. I was surprised that in all those years no one had ever figured out who Lora really was, but Colt pointed out that the kidnapping had occurred on the other side of the country and the adoption, while somewhat nontraditional, probably had seemed legal to the adopting parents. Colt figured that someone—and he was currently trying to find out who that person was—had kidnapped the baby, falsified a birth certificate, and arranged for the adoption through a private firm that was willing to look the other way when it came to verifying custody. What neither of us could figure out was why anyone would kidnap a relatively high-profile baby if the goal wasn't to ask for a ransom.

"Maybe the kidnapper planned to ask for a ransom in the beginning, but something happened and they decided to dump the baby and run," I theorized.

"That thought has occurred to me. It still doesn't explain why Scarlett didn't introduce herself when she saw Lora at the grand opening of the bookstore."

"Are Scarlett and Sophia's birth parents still alive?" I asked.

Colt shook his head. "Both have died. The mother, Olivia, passed away about five years ago and the father, Charles, passed away just two months after Lora was murdered. I haven't been able to find out whether he knew that Scarlett had found Sophia, but it doesn't seem as if she told him. Charles was already very ill with cancer when Lora died."

"So Scarlett inherited the entire estate?"

"Actually, no. Scarlett had a falling-out with her parents at some point and was disinherited shortly before her mother died. The money the couple possessed was Olivia's; she had inherited it from her grandmother, and before she died, Olivia set things up so that the bulk of her estate went into a trust her husband could draw on for the remainder of his life. Once he was gone, the estate went to Sophia, if she was found. If she wasn't found by the time both Olivia and Charles passed, the money went to Olivia's nephew, Jeffery."

"It sounds like Sophia's parents never gave up hope of finding her."

"So it would seem." Colt nodded.

"What do you know of Jeffery? It sounds to me as if Jeffery is the one who benefited from having Sophia out of the way."

Colt picked up a crusty piece of bread and spread soft cheese over it. "I agree. In fact, the timing of his receiving the inheritance was so perfect that it would make me suspect he had a hand in Charles's death, but there was no evidence that his illness was hurried along. After digging around a bit, I found evidence that prior to his inheritance, Jeffery had made some bad investments that landed him in hot water. Inheriting his aunt's millions helped him to get a second shot in life."

"So it really does seem as if Jeffery had a reason not to want Sophia found."

"My current theory is that Scarlett saw Lora at the bookstore opening, realized who she was, and used that information to strike up a deal with Jeffery. She would sit on what she knew until Lora could be taken care of, and in exchange, Jeffery would give a percentage of his inheritance to her."

"Do you think Jeffery was the one to actually kill Lora?" I asked.

"I won't be surprised to find that was exactly what occurred, but of course I can't prove any of this yet, and it is possible Peter was in on things as well. He has to have known that his wife wasn't really visiting a friend, yet that is the story he stuck to. And the fact that he totally seems to have fallen off the face of the earth shortly after Lora's death suggests that he may have left the country."

"Or been killed himself."

"Yes, I suppose there is that possibility. It is true, though, that if the Slavins were having marital problems, Peter might have gone along with things in exchange for enough money to start over somewhere else. He may even have been the one to kill Lora after arranging with Scarlett to provide evidence that Lora was still alive."

I sat back and looked out toward the calm sea. "Okay, it seems like you have a workable theory. Now you just need to figure out how to prove it. Where are Jeffery and Scarlett now?"

"Both live in California, Jeffery in Los Angeles and Scarlett currently in Santa Barbara. I know that proving what I suspect could be difficult, but once I get something concrete to base my theory on, I can probably turn everything over to the FBI and let them close it out."

"So how are you going to get concrete evidence to back up your theory?"

"I have no idea."

It did seem as if proving any of this was going to be close to impossible all these years later. "Why do you think someone went to all the trouble of making you think Lora was still alive?"

"The only thing I can think of is that Scarlett didn't want me opening a murder case that could very well lead to the truth behind Lora's birth, so she, along with, I imagine, Peter and Jeffery, came up with a plan to have Lora disappear. When the neighbor saw Peter kill Lora, Scarlett stepped in to cover for her."

I frowned. "I guess what you are saying makes sense, but it still seems needlessly complicated. Even if Scarlett did recognize Sophia, and even if she realized that she could use Sophia to persuade Jeffery to turn over half his inheritance to her, why involve Peter? Why not just hire someone to kill Lora? Or why kill her at all? Lora had gone her whole life without knowing who she was. The likelihood that she would show up at the eleventh hour to claim her inheritance was pretty small."

"It does seem that the only reason Lora would need to be taken permanently out of the equation would be if there was a real threat that she would appear and ruin things for Jeffery and Scarlett, but so far, I haven't found evidence that she knew who she was or what she might have had coming to her. If she did figure it out, however, Jeffery and Scarlett wanting Sophia dead begins to make sense. Fitting Peter into things is something else entirely."

"This is giving me a headache."

"Right there with you," Colt said.

Once we had exhausted the subject of the murder investigation, the conversation turned toward the absolutely stunning sunset. From there, we discussed other beautiful sights we'd witnessed in our pasts, which led to where in the world we still hoped to go.

"I have always wanted to go to Ireland," I said. "The photos make it seem as if the entire area is so green and lush." I took a sip of my wine. "How about you? Where would you like to visit if you had the time and money to do so?"

"I think probably Australia and New Zealand. I'm not sure why exactly, but the photos I've seen make it look like a beautiful place, and the scuba diving looks to be amazing."

"Do you dive?"

Colt nodded. "I was certified when I was a teen. I used to go often, but then adulthood set in and I got busy. I enjoy my job, but we are a small police force, so it is hard to take time off."

"I've thought about learning to dive. When I was a child, I used to fantasize about being a mermaid. I had an active imagination that allowed me to spend time under the waves, at least in my fantasies."

"You should take the plunge. I know an excellent instructor."

"Maybe once the inn is open and life settles down a bit." I broke off a corner of one of the rich chocolate brownies Colt had brought for dessert and plopped it into my mouth. "Have you always wanted to be a cop?"

Chuckling, Colt admitted that being a cop had been the farthest thing from his mind when he was a kid. "I went through the cowboy phase and I seem to remember there was a time when I dreamed of being a superhero, but the dream I held on to for the longest was that of being a treasure hunter. I had definite plans to travel the world in search of long-lost relics, both in the sea and on land."

"So where did the cop thing come in?"

"I guess it was during my senior year of high school. I'd realized by that point that being a treasure hunter was probably not in the cards and that I needed to figure out what my future would be. I considered college, but I never really liked school. I also knew that I didn't want to get stuck behind a desk. I thought about moving and starting over somewhere, but my friends and my life were here, so I made a list of every job I could think of that would allow me to make a decent income without having to move or go to college, and I came up with either a cop or a fireman. A friend of mine, who has since left Holiday Bay, was working toward a place at the academy, so I decided to follow his lead and signed up as well."

"And is your friend a cop now too?"

Colt shook his head. "He decided that he didn't enjoy getting shot at and is now an accountant. What about you? Did you always want to be a writer?"

I rested my forearms on the table as the sky began to darken. I supposed we should begin to clean up, but Colt had brought a lantern, so we had a few minutes. "I actually wanted to be a private investigator," I said. "I loved mystery stories like Nancy Drew when I was growing up and wanted to be just like her. After I got a little older and realized that being a private investigator was not only dangerous but that the hours were really horrendous, so I decided to write mysteries rather than living them." I leaned back a bit and looked up at the sky. "Don't get me wrong. I still enjoy a good mystery, which is probably why I find myself tagging along after you all the time."

"You have good instincts. You are a great writer, but you may have missed your calling. I think you would have been a fantastic Nancy Drew if you had gone that route."

Chapter 11

Georgia and I talked about it and decided we'd take the whole day off on the Fourth so we could enjoy the local festivities with our friends and neighbors. The day began at the annual pancake breakfast, which wrapped up just about the time the parade was set to begin. We'd considered entering a float for the parade after the huge success of our Easter parade float, but with the grand opening just over a week away, trying to build another float now seemed like too much.

"Oh look, here comes the high school band," Lacy said as music filled the air. She held Maddie in her arms while Lonnie held the hand of each of the four-year-old twins. The triplets stood between them.

"Did you play an instrument, Mommy?" one of the triplets, I think Matthew, asked.

"I did. I wanted to play the drums, but Grandma said she couldn't deal with the noise, so I settled on the flute," Lacy answered.

"I've never seen you play a flute," another of the boys, I thought Michael this time, jumped into the conversation.

"I gave it up after I graduated. I think if I had to do it over again, I would learn to play an instrument that is useful in regular life."

"Like a piano?" the third boy—Mark?—asked.

She nodded. "Yes, exactly like a piano. Your dad plays the guitar and Uncle Colt knows how to play both the keyboard and drums. They play in a band and when we have cookouts at home. If you decide to study an instrument, you might want to learn to play something that will serve you well even when you are no longer part of a marching band."

"I'm going to be in Daddy's band when I grow up," Meghan assured her mother. "I want to sing and play the drums."

"Mommy, look at the dancers," Mary squealed. "I want to be a dancer when I grow up."

When the band got closer it was too loud to converse, so we cheered and clapped our hands. Colt was on duty today, but Tanner and Nikki had joined Georgia and me, who had joined Lonnie and his family, so it was a large group who migrated from the parade to the park where the food fair had been set up.

Lacy, Nikki, and I sat with the kids while Lonnie, Tanner, and Georgia went for the food. The park, as well as the entire downtown section of Holiday Bay, was bursting at the seams with locals and tourists alike, and I could see why the local businesses went to the effort they did to put on these sorts of events.

"It seems like a good turnout," I said to Lacy.

"The events the town holds during the summer and fall are always well attended. Next year you should plan to hold one at the Inn. Maybe music on the lawn or a local art showing. It's a bit of a drive, but I bet something on the bluff would attract a lot of attention."

"I'll consider it. This year I'm just as glad to be a spectator. Well, other than the shift Georgia and I signed up for at the pet adoption clinic."

"I heard you'd agreed to get involved. When will you be working at the clinic?"

"Saturday morning. I met with the coordinator yesterday for a quickie training session. It seems pretty straightforward, and there will be a veteran volunteer working the same shift."

"Be careful that you don't end up coming home with one of the little cuties."

I laughed. "Oh, you don't have to worry about that. The cottage is already pretty crowded with Georgia, Ramos, Rufus, and me."

After the others returned with the food and we'd eaten, Lacy and Lonnie took the kids home for their naps so they wouldn't be too tired to watch the fireworks show that evening. Nikki met up with Jack and the couple headed toward the bandstand to watch the bands, and Georgia went off with Tanner to see to the feeding and exercise of his newest litter of puppies. I thought about either going home or maybe heading over to say hi to Velma, but then I noticed Colt standing near the entrance to the craft fair and decided to head in that direction instead.

"Good turnout," I said.

"Seems about average."

"Have you had to break up any fights or arrest anyone for public intoxication?"

"Not yet, but it's early. The real excitement won't take place until after dark."

"If you are already on duty and plan to still be here during and after the fireworks show, that is going to be a long day."

Colt nodded. "I usually work an eighteen-hour shift during these summertime events. By the end of the weekend I'll be exhausted, but this year I have my vacation to look forward to."

"If you are in town you should plan to come to our wine tasting and jazz festival the last weekend in July."

"The kids and I may be at Disney World that weekend, but if not, I'll try to come. I think you should have a great turnout for the pairing. Personally, I'm looking forward to the beer and brats weekend."

Colt and I chatted a while longer before he got a call to check out a group near the beer garden. I noticed Tessa talking to a woman I was pretty sure I had never met, so I walked in that direction. I figured I'd say hi before heading home to check on Rufus and let Ramos out. In some ways, I still felt that I was living on the fringe of Holiday Bay society, while Georgia was right there in the thick of things. Of course, she had spent a lot more time getting to know people while I tended to remain sequestered away at the estate, writing. Georgia was much more of an extrovert than I was, so it made sense that she knew more people, but I did enjoy my quiet time, so I wasn't sure I would want to take the time she had to cultivate so many new relationships even if I had the time.

******

Velma had called earlier to arrange for Georgia and me to meet her for the fireworks. She'd mentioned that she had a friend who enjoyed digging around in local history and had information for us concerning Emily. I wasn't sure why a gravestone with nothing more than a first name engraved on it had intrigued us as much as it had, but I knew that Trish had exhausted her resources and had come up empty at every turn.

"Abby, Georgia, this is my friend, Izzy."

"Esmeralda actually," the woman explained, "but I prefer Izzy."

After a bit of introductory chitchat, Izzy got right down to business. "I understand that you are researching the Chesterton family and are curious about Emily."

I nodded. "I purchased the estate once lived in by Chamberlain Westminster and his young bride, Abagail Chesterton, which made me curious about her family and, in addition, we met a woman who, as it turns out, is the great-great-granddaughter of Celeste Chesterton, who was in town researching her family tree. Georgia and I went with her to visit the Chesterton family cemetery and noticed the gravestone with the name Emily on it and nothing else."

"We think that she might have been an illegitimate child," Georgia added. "Elizabeth Chesterton's illegitimate child, to be exact."

"We heard from another source that Elizabeth died in childbirth but had not been married at the time," I added.

Izzy chuckled. "I guess this is proof of how rumors get started. Someone thinks they know something and they pass that misinformation on to the next person, who interprets the information in their own way and passes on a somewhat different version of the truth. If I had to guess, you heard about Elizabeth's baby from someone who had heard from a relative who had heard it from their own ancestor."

I nodded. "Yes, that's it exactly. Are you saying that Emily was not Elizabeth's child?"

Izzy's face grew thoughtful. "I suppose in a way Emily *was* Elizabeth's child, but not in the way you're thinking. Emily was a dog. Elizabeth's dog. She died only months after Elizabeth and for reasons I can only guess, the family buried her near the woman who had loved her like a child."

I frowned. "A dog? So Elizabeth didn't die in childbirth?"

"No. Elizabeth was never married, nor was she ever pregnant. Elizabeth died due to an injury she sustained when she went out for a walk and became caught in a freak storm. She fell down a ravine and hit her head. Emily, who had gone along with her, as she always did, went for help after Elizabeth fell and was unable to get up, but by the time Elizabeth was found, she was unconscious. A doctor was called in and he tried to save her, but poor Elizabeth never regained consciousness. Emily, who had been Elizabeth's constant companion since she was a puppy, slipped into a state of depression after the death of her beloved friend. She curled up near Elizabeth's grave and refused to move. She wouldn't eat and simply refused to be lured away. Eventually, Emily passed away and the family buried her next to her beloved human."

I put a hand on my chest. "Oh my. That is so sad."

Izzy nodded. "From what I understand, the family was pretty devastated, which probably explains why Emily's grave is in the family cemetery despite the fact that pets normally aren't buried in family plots."

The sky darkened, and the fireworks began to explode overhead, but I was so fascinated with the knowledge of Chesterton family history that Izzy seemed to possess that I continued to ask questions through the entire show. In the end, Izzy agreed to come out to the estate when she had time. Georgia and I had things we'd found in the attic that seemed to have stories behind them. I hoped that Izzy would know the details of all of them.

Chapter 12

Georgia and I showed up early for the pet adoption clinic on Saturday. We wanted to be sure that we were familiar with the backgrounds and personalities of all the pets waiting to be placed. Lacy hadn't been wrong when she'd warned me against going home with my own furry friend. The puppies and kittens were adorable, but it was a twelve-year-old rescue named Molly who really captured my heart. Not that Georgia and I needed another pet, but when I looked into Molly's big brown eyes that were partially hidden by her long beige bangs, my heart melted.

"Everyone who is interested in adopting one of our charges must fill out an application," the veteran volunteer working with us explained. "The applications are pretty self-explanatory, but if you have any questions, just ask."

"And once the applications are filled out?" I asked.

"They will be reviewed by the shelter owner on Monday. She will call everyone who expressed interest in one of our rescues and let them know if they have been approved as an adoptive parent."

"So the prospective owners won't be able to take the animal they want to adopt home today?" Georgia confirmed.

"Not unless we have interest from someone who has already been approved for adoption," the woman explained. "And there are individuals who have applied and been approved but have not been matched with a dog or cat yet. I have a list of approved humans, so if someone tells you that they have already gone through the application and approval process, just send them to me."

Things did seem pretty straightforward. Once the clinic opened, things began to get very busy very quickly. I did the best I could to answer questions, explain the process, and hand out applications. I hoped all the dogs and cats would find homes, though I really hoped that Molly, a terrier mix of some sort that probably didn't weigh much more than Rufus, would find a loving human who would be patient with an aging dog. I didn't know a lot about pets, but I was sure no animal should have to live out their final years behind bars.

Georgia and I had been assigned to work from nine to noon, although we'd arrived at eight. By the time our shift ended, we had a stack of applications, and several of the dogs and cats had gone home with preapproved adoptive parents.

"Did anyone apply to adopt Molly?" I asked after we'd been released from our commitment.

"No, I'm afraid not," the woman who seemed to be in charge replied. "It is hard to place dogs and cats once they reach a certain age."

I glanced at the timid little dog who simply stared at me with sad eyes. "I'd like to apply to adopt her."

The woman raised a brow. "Are you sure? I know that these clinics have a way of tugging at your heartstrings, but when we approve someone to adopt one of our rescues, we assume they are interested in a lifetime commitment."

I nodded. "I'm sure."

The woman's eyes softened. "Look, I really appreciate you helping out today and I can see that you feel sorry for Molly, but I don't feel confident that you have thought this out. Why don't you take Molly home for a trial? Call the shelter on Monday. I'm working from ten to two. If you still want to adopt Molly, I'll take care of the paperwork, but if you have changed your mind after having had time to really think about it, we will take her back, no questions asked."

"Okay," I agreed. "I think that is a good plan."

I was given a leash and a travel crate to borrow. I loaded the crate in the car, and then Molly and I headed to the food court to meet up with Georgia, who had gone on ahead to meet Nikki. I paused when I realized how crowded the area was. I looked down at Molly. "What do you think? Are you cool with the crowd?"

Molly looked up at me, her huge brown eyes meeting mine. She wagged her tail as if to assure me that if it was cool with me, it was cool with her. I looked around until I found Georgia and Nikki sitting on a picnic bench with Lacy and her six children. Molly and I headed in their direction.

"You brought Molly." Georgia smiled.

"She will be staying with us this weekend for a trial," I responded, trying to ignore the look on Lacy's face that seemed to scream *I told you so*.

"Can we pet her?" Matthew asked.

I glanced at Lacy.

"It's fine with me, but be gentle. Molly is with strange people in a strange environment and we don't want to scare her," Lacy cautioned her five older children, who all wanted a turn to pet the adorable little dog.

I watched Molly closely for any signs of distress, but she must have lived with children in the past because rather than being scared, she seemed to be delighted with the attention.

"It seems like she is a pretty mellow dog," Nikki noted. "A lot of dogs get grouchy as they age, but Molly seems to be totally chill. Are you going to keep her?"

I nodded. "That is the plan. The woman from the shelter wanted Molly and me to have a chance to get to know each other before we made the paperwork permanent. I guess I'll have to see how she gets along with Rufus and Ramos, but Ramos gets along with everyone and Rufus is okay with dogs. Molly isn't all that much larger than he is, and she is pretty quiet, so I anticipate that they will get along just fine as long as Molly is willing to accept the fact that Rufus has dibs on the extra pillow when it comes time to settle in for the night."

"If you keep adopting animals, you are going to need a bigger bed," Georgia teased.

"Maybe, but my two fur babies together are only half as big as your one monster dog." I glanced at Lacy. "Where is Lonnie?"

"Lonnie, Colt, and Tanner went to buy a bag full of corndogs and fries for the kids. I think they planned to pick up barbecue beef sandwiches for the adults." She looked toward the food court. "They are still in line for the corndogs, so if you want a sandwich, you have time to let them know."

"I'll text Colt to ask him to pick up a sandwich for me," I said. "Do you plan to spend the afternoon in town?"

"We are going to eat and then let the kids play some of the games at the kiddie carnival. I think they will be ready for naps after that."

"How about the two of you?" I looked at Nikki and Georgia.

"I have a date with Jack when he gets off work at three," Nikki explained.

"And I was planning to hang out with you," Georgia informed me. "We can stay as long as you want, or I am fine with heading home after we eat if you prefer."

I looked down at Molly. "I will probably head home and get Molly settled. I wanted to finish up the flyers we're distributing at the grand opening highlighting our fall special events so we can get them to the printer on Monday."

"I thought you already had your flyers done," Lacy said.

"We do, but Georgia and I decided that it wasn't too early to begin advertising the events we have planned for September and October. The local printer said he could print the flyers in one day once we got him a final proof. I'd like to get that to him by Monday."

"Are you still doing the haunted inn thing for Halloween?" Nikki asked.

I nodded. "We have a Halloween-themed event for every weekend in October. I am really looking forward to the entire month. I've heard how lovely fall in New England can be and can't wait for the trees to change and the air to grow crisp."

"You might want to order your pumpkins ahead of time if you are going to need a bunch," Lacy suggested. "There are distributors who will deliver, and if you don't plan ahead, you might not get the best-quality gourds."

"It would be fun to set up a pumpkin patch," Nikki said. "Of course, the pumpkins in your patch won't actually be attached to a vine, but you can arrange them to look as if they grew in the ground. Throw in some hay bales and scarecrows and you'll have a fun October theme."

Georgia and I both agreed that planning ahead and ordering in advance was going to be key if we wanted to stay on top of the changing seasons and plethora of holidays.

After the guys returned with the food, the topic of conversation migrated toward a sunset picnic and a bonfire at the beach. Those gathered agreed that a weekday would work best, but because Lonnie and Colt worked then, a Friday in July was offered as an alternate date. The following Friday would be a busy one for Georgia and me because we had the grand opening on Saturday, so other dates were tossed around until we realized that the first Friday everyone had open was well into August.

"How are things going with the Slavin case?" I asked Colt when Lonnie and Lacy and their children had headed off to the kiddie carnival, Nikki had gone to talk to some friends, and Tanner and Georgia had left to check out the bands.

"As we discussed before, while we had come up with what seems to be a plausible theory without proof, I really had nothing, but I think I might have found something that could provide leverage to get Scarlett to talk."

"You think that she will confess?"

"With the right motivation. If the theory that she recognized Sophia and then used her knowledge of her twin's whereabouts to convince Jeffery to give her a chunk of the inheritance he would receive as long as Sophia stayed out of the picture is correct, all we need to do is prove that Scarlett knew about the plan to kill Sophia. I still don't know if Jeffery, Peter, or some third party murdered Lora, but I'm hoping if we can rattle Scarlett, we can get her to narc on whoever did the actual killing."

"It occurred to me to wonder why Scarlett was even in Holiday Bay when the bookstore opened. At the time she lived in Malibu, California, so the fact that she was here was most likely because she was either passing through or she was here to visit someone who lived here. I supposed either could be true, but when you add in the fact that Lora's body was buried so far north of here, I thought it might be possible that she knew someone who lived in the area where Lora's body was buried. Maybe someone from there was the murderer."

"I had a similar thought, so I did some checking and found out that the woman who was standing next to Scarlett in the photo you found in the newspaper is a high school teacher who lives in the same small town where Lora's body was found. Her name is Stephanie Askew. She attended the same college as Scarlett and when I spoke to her, she verified that at the time of the bookstore opening, Scarlett was in this area to hang out with her for a couple of days. The man standing next to Stephanie is Evan Trout, a laborer from the same small town where Stephanie lives. He has been in and out of jail for the past ten years for mostly minor offenses such as car theft and assault while intoxicated. I have an appointment to have another conversation with Stephanie tomorrow. I'm hoping she will have stayed in touch with Scarlett and will know whether Scarlett recognized Sophia while she was visiting Holiday Bay. Ultimately, I'm hoping she can tell me something I can use for leverage to get Scarlett to tell me what she knows about Lora's death. I am beginning to suspect that if Peter wasn't the killer, it might have been Trout."

I frowned. "Are you still thinking that Scarlett is the mastermind behind this whole thing?"

"Perhaps. It still makes sense to me that Scarlett recognized Sophia at the bookstore opening and stored that piece of information away in her mind. After her father got sick, she must have realized that Jeffery was going to receive her mother's money, so she went to him with what she knew. She probably traded her silence for a piece of the action. Not wanting to leave things up to chance, she might have decided to kill Sophia, so she either enlisted the help of Peter or Trout. Initially, I thought that Jeffery might be the killer, but the more I think about it, the less convinced I am that that particular part of the theory is accurate."

"So you are hoping that Trout or Stephanie will know something that might help you prove things and be willing to tell you about it?"

Colt nodded.

"What time will you be heading north?"

"At around ten. We are supposed to meet at around noon after she gets home for from her kid's soccer game."

"I would be willing to come along for the ride if you want company."

Colt nodded. "I'd like that."

Chapter 13

Ramos adored Molly, and while Rufus wasn't quite as enamored, it appeared he was going to tolerate her just fine. Georgia and I took both dogs for a walk along the bluff. Ramos was the sort to trudge along slowly due to his large size, which was perfect for Molly, because she not only had short legs but, at her age, it seemed her gait had slowed to a waddle on the best of days.

"I think that Molly is going to fit right in," Georgia said. "Although I am surprised you wanted to take on another animal to care for."

"I just felt so sorry for the poor little thing. Here she is, at the end years of her life, and she is stuck living at the shelter because everyone wants a puppy or at least a young dog. I know she probably won't be with us for all that long, but I figure that we can make the last years of her life some of the best years of her life."

Georgia hugged me. "I totally agree, and I love the idea of adopting a senior dog. And I can help with the trips outdoors and whatever else you need. She seems to be really well-behaved. Do you know how she ended up in the shelter?"

I nodded. "I read her file when we first arrived at the adoption event. Her owner died a couple of months ago and his daughter didn't want Molly. No one seemed to want to take on the responsibility for a dog with arthritis and partial hearing loss, so she ended up at the shelter. I realize that the medical bills might be more than they would be for a younger dog, but I can afford that and when she looked at me with those big brown eyes, I was hooked."

"Ramos is a big lug who sleeps away most of the day. He'll enjoy having Molly to curl up with." Georgia looked out toward the sea. "It's going to be a lovely evening. We should take a bottle of wine and some cheese and crackers out to the deck and watch the day wane. We can go over our to-do list while we relax."

"That sounds like a wonderful idea. I'll bring out one of the big floor pillows for Molly to lay on. I suspect she will appreciate the padding."

"Just don't take the blue one that Rufus prefers. He might seem like he is fine with Molly, but I have a feeling that if she moves in on his territory, he might get downright jealous."

"We can bring out pillows for all three animals."

When we returned to the cottage, Georgia assembled the light meal while I lugged out the pillows onto the deck. I figured Ramos would be just as happy on his dog bed, so I lugged that outside as well. Once everyone was settled, I curled into a deck chair and sipped the chilled wine. I had a million things to do during the next week, but at that moment, I felt more relaxed and contented than I had in a long while. It might be the excellent view, the happy animals, or the wonderful friend who felt more like a sister, but as the sun began to descend toward the horizon beyond the bluff, I realized that the serenity I'd longed for when I made the trip east had found me and settled in along the way.

Georgia sat down on the chair next to me and held up her glass. "Here is to the million little things we have to be thankful for."

"Hear, hear."

"Can you believe the grand opening is just a week away? I feel like it was just yesterday I rolled into your drive looking for work and you very kindly invited me into your home and your life."

"It does feel like the whole thing has sort of snuck up on us."

Georgia reached out, took my hand, and gave it a squeeze. "When Ramos and I showed up on your doorstep, we had nothing more than each other and a half-broken-down truck. Now we have a home and a family. I know I've thanked you before, but I want you to know how much I appreciate everything you have done for us."

"Inviting you in was the best decision I have ever made." Rufus jumped into my lap. "Well, I suppose the second-best decision, after allowing this huge beast to bully me into letting him stay when I'd been so determined that he wouldn't."

Georgia chuckled. "Rufus does have a way of getting what he wants."

I glanced at Molly, who was fast asleep on her pillow. I knew that she didn't have a lot of years left, but I hoped we could make her happy while she was with us.

"Did I tell you the florist called and wanted to know if we wanted flowers for the suites? At first, I didn't think we should bother, because no one would be staying in the suites—well, other than Annie and Artie—but then I realized that the point of the open house was to show off what we've created, so I went ahead and ordered flowers for all the rooms. It is an extra expense, but I think it will help the rooms feel finished if you know what I mean."

I nodded. "I do, and I agree. I think that flowers are an important element of the vibe we are trying to create. On a previous visit, I spoke to the florist about black and orange carnations for the Halloween events. It seems you can get carnations in pretty much any color you want. She suggested black roses for the dining table as well, which I think will add a spooky feel to the room."

"I'm glad you brought up Halloween," Georgia said. "I met a woman today who is part of a community theater group. She told me that her group would be willing to do a murder mystery dinner party for our guests. They don't charge for the service, but they accept donations, which they use to purchase costumes and props."

"I love that idea. Do they ask for participation from the guests?"

"Sort of. The group acts out all the main parts, but they ask the guests to help out with minor parts where learning lines is not a factor. It is all on a volunteer basis, so anyone who simply wants to watch is assigned a role like Dinner Guest Number Two, and all they do is observe. It sounds like a lot of fun and it would be a lot less work than trying to write our own mystery, which was something we discussed."

"I think you're right. Let's see what we need to do to make a reservation with them."

"Tanner said he hired them to do a fund-raiser a couple of years ago and he thought they did a good job. We can choose to do a weekend or a dinner event, but I'm thinking we might want to start with a dinner."

"Agreed. Did the group we asked to do the pumpkin carving demonstration for one of our Saturday-on-the-lawn events confirm?"

Georgia shook her head. "Not yet. I'll call them on Monday." She took a bite of the cheese she had picked up at the local cheese and wine shop. "This is really good. It is sharp but mild enough not to leave an aftertaste."

"We should offer a cheese tasting at our wine and jazz event," I suggested.

"That's a good idea. I'll see if I can line something up."

Georgia and I continued to chat about our plans for the upcoming months as the sun dipped into the sea. I had come to Holiday Bay a broken woman, and while I still had moments of sadness, in general, I felt that in the course of restoring the inn, I had restored and renewed my life.

Chapter 14

I was up and ready when Colt came to pick me up the following morning. Georgia planned to take both Molly and Ramos for a nice, long walk along the bluff and promised to keep an eye on the newest addition to our family while I was away so that I didn't need to worry about her being alone in the house on her first full day with us. I wasn't even sure why I'd offered to tag along with Colt. It wasn't as if he needed my help, and I certainly had plenty of other things to tend to, but I enjoyed spending time with him, and a long drive north seemed like a good opportunity.

"By the way, I meant to tell you that I received an official letter from the Internal Affairs department of the San Francisco Police Department, letting know that some of Ben's files had been looked at, but they hadn't found any wrongdoing and the investigation was closed."

"I guess that's a good thing."

I nodded. "It is. I'm glad that Ben's actions and decisions are no longer under review, but I will admit that after having looked through his files, I have my own questions." I turned so that I was facing Colt more directly. "You were going to look into a few of the case files Ben brought home. Did you ever find anything?"

Colt shifted his hands on the wheel. "Yes and no. I did stumble across some interesting facts, but I can't say that I found any smoking guns."

"Interesting facts?"

Colt slowed as he approached a car plodding along at five miles an hour under the speed limit. "Remember the cop whose throat had been slit and was left in an alley to die?"

"Yeah, I remember. The murder took place during the day, yet the investigating officer couldn't find a single witness who would admit to seeing what had gone down."

"We discussed the fact that while the cop was on duty and should have been patrolling his area, his body was found clear across the city, where he had no business being."

"So, did you find out anything new?"

"Maybe. I don't have all the facts, but I did find out that the cop who died was partnered with Frank Ribaldie before he was assigned to narcotics and then eventually to homicide."

I frowned. "It seems like Frank's name has come up a lot. He worked out of the same precinct as Ben, but I still wonder why Ben would have files relating to cases in which Frank was involved that date so far back. Do you think that Frank was in some way responsible for his partner's death and Ben knew it and was trying to gather proof?"

"Probably not, but I suppose it is possible, and I did find that Frank was the dead man's partner interesting. Having said that, we have already discussed the fact that now that Ben's name has been cleared, it might be best to leave things alone."

"But if there is something illegal going on…"

"There probably isn't. I know I just said that I found some interesting facts, but interesting does not necessarily equate to wrongdoing." Colt turned slightly to glance at me. He must have noticed my frown because he continued with his thought. "You told me that Ben was a good cop who would never take bribes or be involved with any other sort of illegal activity. Did you mean that?"

"Yes, of course."

"So, if Ben was being investigated by Internal Affairs and he turned out to be clean, it stands to reason the other men under investigation might be innocent of wrongdoing as well."

I supposed Colt had a point. "But what about the fact that Frank was looking for a file and then my storage unit was broken in to?"

"Frank emailed you looking for a file, but that doesn't mean he was guilty of doing anything wrong, or that he was the one who broke into your storage unit. We went into this looking for red flags, so given that alone, the fact that we found some shouldn't be surprising. Yes, it does seem like a coincidence that Ben had a file pertaining to the unsolved murder of the partner of a man he was currently working with, but that doesn't make Frank guilty of anything. We'd need to have a lot more information than we currently do even to determine why Ben had the file."

Again, Colt had made a good point. "So you think we should just let it go?"

Colt nodded. "I think the best thing for you to do is to be grateful that Ben's name was cleared and to move on with your life. You are building something special in Holiday Bay. Now that Ben's name has been cleared, I see no reason to muddy the waters worrying about some random files that we can't understand the significance of. At least we can't understand the significance without a whole lot more information."

"Yeah, okay, I get what you are saying. And I do have a lot going on right now. What do you think I should do with Ben's files?"

"I'd keep them just in case this comes around again, but I'd file them away somewhere out of the way."

"Okay. I'll do that. Thanks."

"No problem. I am always happy to help. I figure I owe you for all the times you've helped me."

I couldn't help but grin. "I guess we make a good team. Does the woman we are on our way to meet know why you want to speak to her?"

"She knows that I am looking for some information regarding Scarlett. I didn't fill her in beyond that. She did say that she hadn't seen Scarlett in years, but I assured her it was their acquaintance in the past I was interested in."

Stephanie lived on a tree-lined street of older homes with quaint charm. The yards were large and well-maintained and the houses, while small, were kept up, most recently painted. The roses that lined the front walkway seemed to offer a greeting of welcome as soon as we pulled up along the front curb.

"You must be Chief Wilder," a woman with shoulder-length blond hair said as soon as she opened the front door.

"I am." Colt turned to me. "This is my associate, Abby Sullivan."

The woman stepped aside. "Come on in. My girls are in the family room with some friends, so I thought we'd chat on the patio."

Colt said that would be fine, and I found the patio to be as charming and welcoming as the front yard.

"Your flowers are gorgeous," I said, taking a seat at the umbrella-covered table.

"Thank you. Gardening is a passion of mine." She turned to Colt. "You want to ask me about Scarlett Brookvale?"

Colt nodded. "She's a person of interest in one of the cases I am working on. I understand that you have known her for quite some time."

Stephanie nodded. "Scarlett and I were in the same sorority in college, so I'd say we met almost twenty years ago."

"Were you close?"

She shrugged. "I guess you could say we were close, although we had little in common except for our love of partying, at least at the time. I wish I could say that I took college seriously, but I didn't. I really didn't even want to go to college, but my parents offered me an ultimatum: either go to college and obtain a degree in the field of my choice or stay home and take over my mother's flower shop. I was not at all interested in running the shop, so I went to college."

"Did you graduate?"

"I did, even though I was not a serious student. After graduation, I was pretty lost and had absolutely no idea what I wanted to do with my life, so I ended up moving home and taking over my mother's flower shop, which was what she'd wanted me to do in the first place."

"And Scarlett?" Colt asked.

"Scarlett was from a wealthy family. Her mother insisted that she go to college, but she never took it seriously. She knew she had an inheritance in her future and was never going to need to work. I'm afraid she acted accordingly."

"Acted accordingly?" Colt asked.

"While she was in school, she received an allowance that she used to establish a reputation as a spoiled heiress without a single intact brain cell to aid in her decision-making. In other words, she was a hot mess, but she was rich and beautiful, so she was a popular hot mess. She dropped out after her junior year and went back to California, where she spent most of her time being seen at the most sought-after parties and clubs. We weren't in touch during that time of her life because she was either drunk or hung over most of the time. When she turned thirty, Scarlett treated herself and some of her worthless friends to a huge party in Vegas. I understand she spent a small fortune in a very short period of time and, even worse, dragged her family's name through the mud while doing so. Her mom was enraged and cut her off to fend for herself. Scarlett had no marketable skills, nor did she have any desire to find a legitimate job, so she drifted around between friends for a while. By 2013, I guess she had blown through her West Coast friends, so she showed up on my doorstep and announced that she was in Maine for a visit. I wasn't thrilled to see her, but I wasn't looking for conflict either, so I allowed her to stay with me for a while. I showed her around, which is how we ended up in Holiday Bay on the day of that bookstore opening."

"And you noticed Sophia as well?" Colt asked.

"Yes, of course. I asked Scarlett about her and she told me that the woman who looked exactly like her was a cousin she'd had a falling-out with and didn't want to talk to. We were only in the crowd watching for a minute before Scarlett insisted we leave."

"And how long did she stay with you?"

"With me, just two weeks. But I'd introduced her to a friend, and he invited her to crash with him. She ended up staying with him until her mom died in 2014. She left Maine at that point. I think she figured she was going to get some big inheritance, but she didn't. When her mom cut her off, she cut her off completely, though she was able to persuade her dad to reinstate her allowance. I haven't seen her again since she left Maine, but I'm pretty sure that Evan went to California to hang out with her a few times."

"So at no point did Scarlett say or do anything that would lead you to believe that the woman you saw at the bookstore opening was actually her twin sister?" Colt confirmed.

"Scarlett had a twin sister?"

"She did, but the sisters were separated when they were infants."

Stephanie frowned. "So the woman at the bookstore was her sister?"

Colt nodded.

"She didn't say anything to me about a sister. When I pointed out that the woman who was standing in the front of the bookstore with the owner looked like her, she just shrugged and fed me the estranged-cousin story. That is so weird. Do you think the sister knew who Scarlett was?"

"As far as we can tell, she didn't even see Scarlett. If she did, she didn't mention it to anyone that we know of."

"So this woman, the sister, she's dead?"

"Yes," Colt verified. "She was murdered three years ago."

"And you think that Scarlett was involved?"

Colt paused before answering. "We think she might have been. We are still putting together the information we have. From what you know of Scarlett, do you think she's capable of murder?"

"Sure. If money was involved. Scarlett and I weren't close after college, but even then it seemed that for her, the world revolved around spending money and living the life she felt she was entitled to."

"And Evan? Do you think he could have been persuaded to become involved in a murder conspiracy?" Colt asked.

Stephanie hesitated. "Maybe. Evan didn't care about money as much as Scarlett did, but he was really into her. If she asked him to help her murder someone, my inclination is to say that he would have."

"Do you know where we might find him?" Colt asked.

Stephanie shook her head. "He took off a few years ago. I haven't seen him since. I suppose if he helped Scarlett kill her sister, he might have decided it was a good idea to disappear."

"Does he have family or close friends who might know where he is?"

"He has a sister, Giovanna. She lives in Vermont; I'm not sure where. She is married, so I'm not even sure about her last name. She wasn't really close to him, so I don't know if she would know where he was now, but I suppose if anyone would, it would be her." Stephanie paused. "You might want to speak to a man named Hugh Donaldson. Hugh and Evan were pretty tight, so he might know where he went off to. Hugh owns a local garage. I'm not sure he will be there today, but he might. The garage is right on the corner of Second and Maple. You can't miss it."

"And the name of the garage?" Colt asked.

"Hugh's Auto Repair."

We spoke with Stephanie for a while longer and then headed to the garage. We hoped Hugh would be in so we wouldn't need to spend a lot of time tracking him down. We'd asked Stephanie if he kept regular hours, and according to her, he tended to work when he had customers lined up and close things down when he didn't.

Hugh Donaldson turned out to be a large man. He was six feet ten inches at least, broad-shouldered, and wide-chested. He spoke with a booming voice, and the scars on his face made him look like a thug I would never want to run in to in a dark alley, but after a while, I could see that he was actually a pretty nice guy.

Colt introduced himself and then asked Hugh if he would be willing to answer a few questions. Hugh nodded and led us to a very greasy break room. I looked around for a marginally clean place to sit, then sort of perched on the edge of a seat to minimize the damage to my pants.

"I understand you are friends with Evan Trout."

The man nodded. "Yeah, that's right. Is Evan in some sort of trouble?"

"He is wanted for questioning in regard to a case I am working on. Do you know where I can find him?"

"Rio."

"Rio de Janeiro?" Colt asked.

Hugh nodded. "He came into some money a while back and left Maine. I haven't seen him since, but he called me a week ago looking for a lockbox he left with me. He mentioned that he was calling from Rio."

"Lockbox?" Colt asked.

"A big trunk with some of his stuff in it. It was too big to take with him when he left, so I told him I'd store it in my shed."

"Is it still there?" Colt asked.

"For now. Evan told me that someone would be coming by for it within a few weeks."

"Do you mind if we take a look?"

Hugh shrugged. "It's okay by me, but keep in mind that all I've done is store a trunk for a friend. If there is a dead body inside, I had nothing to do with it."

"Dead body?" Colt asked. "Is there a reason you think there could be a dead body inside?"

Hugh hesitated.

"If you know something, it would be best to cooperate."

Hugh blew out a breath. "Evan brought the trunk by three years ago. He said he needed to leave town and wanted me to store some of his stuff. He offered to pay me two hundred dollars a month to store the trunk, so I agreed. The thing is that when Evan dropped the trunk off, he had dried blood on his hands. He'd tried to wash it off, but he wasn't able to get it all. I asked him about it and he said he'd cut his arm. He showed me a gash, so his story was believable, but if I am completely honest, I have always wondered if the blood on his hands really was from trying to stop the flow from the gash on his arm or something a bit more sinister."

Colt stood up. "Well, you have my interest. Let's take a look."

As it turned out, the trunk did not hold a body, but it did contain a knife with blood on it, bloody gloves, a piece of plastic, and several bloody towels. Colt loaded the trunk and its contents in his car. If the blood matched Lora's, which we were sure it would, it seemed as if we'd at least found her killer. Trying to prove that Scarlett was in on Lora's death would require additional evidence, and we still had no idea if Peter was involved in the murder or if he was an additional victim, but at least we had a place to start and probably enough to get the FBI involved.

Chapter 15

As the grand opening grew closer, so did my anxiety. I could see that Georgia had everything handled and knew I should relax, but it felt as if everything I had worked for over the past eight months had come down to this single event, and no matter how hard I tried, I simply couldn't let go and enjoy it. It helped that both Rufus and Molly wanted to cuddle that morning, so instead of getting out of bed the moment I woke up, I lingered with my furry friends.

"My sister, Annie, will be here tomorrow," I said to them. "I plan to introduce you, but she isn't the sort to appreciate the value of a furry companion, so don't take it personally if she isn't as enamored with you as I've grown to be."

Rufus began to purr. He curled into my lap when I sat up and leaned against the headboard, while Molly put her head on the part of my leg not occupied by Rufus. I ran my hand through the thick fur of both my companions and felt my stress melt away. By the time I finally decided to peel myself out of bed, I felt confident and relaxed. Today would be a busy one. Trish was scheduled to arrive, and Nikki planned to come by to help Georgia and me. I knew there would be tense moments, but deep down inside, I knew that everything was going to turn out exactly as I had envisioned. Of course, there is a risk in overconfidence, which I was soon to find out.

"I have news," Georgia said as soon as I walked out of my bedroom.

I took a deep breath. "Good news?"

"Not exactly. It seems that the delivery truck carrying the dozens of bouquets we ordered has been in an accident."

"The driver?"

"Fine, but the flowers were ruined."

Okay, I would not panic. The flower arrangements were important, but we had twenty-four hours to replace them. I asked Georgia what our options were.

"The florist has flowers in stock to redo the larger pieces for the outdoor tables where we're serving the food, but we will have to be flexible as to the type and color."

Flexible. I could do that. We might not be able to pull off the exact effect we'd hoped for, but it would still be nice. I hoped. "And the flowers for the inn itself?"

"Nikki and Tanner are heading to Portland to pick up as many flowers as they can get their hands on. The flower shop I found has a good selection, but they have a huge wedding tomorrow, so they don't have the manpower to do the arrangements. I made a few calls, and we have volunteers coming by to help out as soon as Tanner and Nikki get back. We may end up with something different from what we had in mind, but I'm sure it will still be lovely."

I swallowed hard. "Okay," I said in the calmest voice I could manage. "Anything else?"

"The tablecloths we ordered were supposed to be white. They're purple."

"Purple?"

"I called the rental company to inform them of the error. They apologized and are going to see if they can find white in time to switch them out by tomorrow, but to be honest, they didn't sound all that confident of being able to do so. If they can find white tablecloths in time, we will be fine, but if they can't, which I think is likely, we can either use the purple or try to find white somewhere else."

I thought about our lovely red, white, and blue theme. "Let's look for white. Maybe we can find some in Portland and Nikki and Tanner can pick them up when they pick up the flowers."

Georgia nodded. I noticed for the first time that she looked as if she was going to cry.

"I'm so sorry," she said. "I should have been on top of this. I promised you everything would be perfect and it isn't."

I stepped forward and hugged my best friend. "None of this is your fault and whether we have white tablecloths or purple, and whether we have perfectly matching bouquets or a hodgepodge of flowers, it will still be perfect."

Georgia squeezed me with her arms. "Thank you for understanding. I really want tomorrow to be the day you have been envisioning all these months."

"It will be." I took a step back. "Let's check the dishware, wineglasses, and other items that were delivered yesterday to make sure we don't have any other minor emergencies to deal with."

Georgia headed across the yard to the inn to check everything she hadn't already and to recheck everything she had. I poured myself a cup of coffee and headed out onto the deck. I was determined to try to enjoy the weekend and I knew that in order to do that I needed to let go of the little things I couldn't control and in the end really wouldn't make a difference. Ramos followed me out onto the deck with Molly on his heels. They both stretched out in the sun to enjoy the warmth of the early morning rays. Rufus had been eating his breakfast when I'd headed out, but I was sure he would be along when he was done.

I closed my eyes and listened to the sound of the sea crashing onto the rocks below. I loved the steady rhythm of the pounding waves. I let my mind relax as I pictured the grand opening. After Ben died, I'd tried focused meditation in an attempt to center my mind and quiet the chaos. It hadn't worked then, but perhaps I could extrapolate those skills and apply them to this situation. I was picturing myself mingling among family and friends on the new lawn the gardener had so recently laid when my phone rang, ruining the mood.

"Good morning, Velma," I answered in a cheery voice.

"Abby. I just spoke to Georgia. The poor thing was frantic about flowers and tablecloths. I told her I'd be by later to help with the flowers. In the meantime, I called the church, and they have fifteen large white tablecloths they use for special events that they are happy to lend you."

I exhaled slowly. "That is really great, Velma. I know Georgia has been frantic since she found out the rental company sent purple instead of white. I can pick them up if you can let me know who I should ask for."

"Colt was here for breakfast when I called, so he volunteered to pick them up and drop them off."

"That was nice of him, but I know how busy he is. I really don't mind picking them up."

"I don't think Colt would have volunteered if he didn't have the time. Besides, now that he has wrapped up the murder he was working on, it seems as if he has time to spare."

"He wrapped it up?"

"Thanks to the items in the trunk that man left behind. Listen, I have customers to see to. Just pass the message about the tablecloths on to Georgia. I tried to call her myself, but it went straight to voice mail."

"Okay, I'll tell her, and thanks, Velma."

As soon as I hung up, I headed over to the main house, where Georgia was unpacking boxes. There were stacks of blue plates, red napkins, and etched wineglasses with our logo stacked on the back counter. The red umbrellas brought a splash of color to the patio area right off the bat, as did the red, white, and blue flowers we'd planted in the flower boxes.

"Velma arranged to borrow fifteen white tablecloths from the church," I informed Georgia.

Her facial muscles visibly relaxed. "Really? That's wonderful. Tanner called to say that they were able to get quite a few red, white, and blue flowers as long as we were willing to count dark purple as blue."

"That should work," I confirmed.

"The flower shop is remaking the centerpieces for the serving tables, so we should be back in business." Georgia smiled for the first time that morning.

"Did the wine that was donated arrive?" I wondered.

Georgia nodded. "The red is stacked in the pantry and the white is chilling. I also purchased soft drinks as well as beer, and of course, we will serve punch to those with a sweet tooth."

I picked up one of the flyers Georgia had set on the large dining table for distribution at the opening. There was a photo of the inn on the cover, but the porch and the yard in front of the building had been decorated with pumpkins, scarecrows, and even a ghost. "These are really great. I know if I saw this flyer I would want to visit that house for Halloween."

"I thought they turned out well. I have regular flyers in addition to the seasonal ones. I really think that we are going to be booked to capacity by the end of the weekend."

"I hope so. I wonder if we should have purchased a guest book. If we asked people to sign in and leave an email, we could follow up with a newsletter."

Georgia crossed the room and started rooting through a box. She held up a leather-bound book. "I have one. I'm glad you reminded me. With everything that is going on, I can see that I might very well have forgotten to put it out." Georgia put her hands on her hips and looked around the room. "I think I am going to call all the food vendors I ordered supplies from to confirm the orders as well as the delivery time. I'm not sure I can handle another open-house disaster."

I wasn't sure that damaged flowers and the wrong color tablecloths should be labeled disasters, but I got where Georgia was coming from. I'd hired her eight months ago as an inn manager. To this point, she really hadn't had anything to manage despite the fact that she had helped a lot. I knew she wanted tomorrow to be perfect, and for her sake, I really hoped it was.

I heard a car in the drive and headed outside. Colt was just pulling up with the borrowed tablecloths. I opened his back door and began carrying them inside.

"Velma said you closed out the Lora Slavin case," I said as we both returned for a second trip.

"I did. The blood on the knife we found in the trunk turned out to be Lora's, and there was blood on her nightgown belonging to her and to another person. Given the case I made that the killer was most likely Evan, they subpoenaed his medical records and found his DNA in the system. When they realized the blood on the nightgown that did not belong to Lora belonged to him, they issued a warrant for his arrest. Of course, he is not currently on the radar and is most likely out of the country as Hugh indicated, so I don't know when or even if he will be found and held accountable, but the warrant gave the FBI leverage to convince Jeffery to confess his part in the conspiracy."

"And what was his part exactly?" I asked.

"As we suspected, Scarlett recognized Sophia at the bookstore opening and sat on that information until her father was on his deathbed. When she realized that when he died everything in her mother's estate would go to Jeffery and her allowance would dry up, she went to him and told him that she knew where Sophia was, and that if he didn't want her to tell her father, thereby nullifying his inheritance, he had to agree to give her a big chunk of everything he inherited. He agreed, but he didn't want the risk of Sophia showing up one day and muddying the water, so Scarlett assured him she'd take care of it."

"So, based on what we learned, what she did to 'take care of it' was to convince a lovestruck Evan Trout to kill Lora and dump the body where no one would ever find it."

"Exactly."

"Where did Peter fit into all this?"

"He didn't," Colt answered. "Or at least I don't think he was part of it. I still haven't tracked him down. It appears that he really was at the conference he'd told me he'd attended during the week his wife died. The couple had been having problems and he knew his wife planned to file for divorce, so it appears to me as if he actually believed that his wife had left town. I'm not sure why she didn't go, if that is what she had planned to do, but one of Lora's friends told me that she had been having an affair and most likely had only told Peter that she was going to be visiting a friend so she wouldn't arouse his suspicion if she spent time with her lover."

"So when you called Peter after Erica saw her being murdered and he told you that his wife was out of town visiting a friend, you think that he believed that to be the truth?"

"Yes. That is how it seems."

"How did the conversation you had with Scarlett occur?"

"When I called Peter about the attack Erica told me she had seen, he gave me Lora's cell, and when I called it, Scarlett answered and agreed to a video chat to prove she was alive and well. The woman I chatted with looked like Lora which was enough to convince me that Erica hadn't seen what she thought she had."

"Yes, but how did Scarlett get hold of Lora's cell?"

Colt shrugged. "I guess Evan must have given it to her after he killed her."

I paused and let the entire thing roll around in my mind. "So it sounds like Scarlett was the mastermind behind the whole thing."

Colt nodded. "That's my take on it. There is an APB out for her arrest. She hasn't been at home, but I'm sure she'll be found."

"So Jeffery has been arrested, Scarlett is MIA, and Evan is out of the country, perhaps in Rio?"

Colt nodded. "As I said, I don't know what happened to Peter, but I suspect he is dead. If I had to guess, once he arrived home and found his wife gone he became a liability and Scarlett had him taken care of."

Talk about a piece of work. I couldn't imagine someone would kill two people over money, especially if one of them was her sister. No wonder her mother had disinherited her. When I'd first heard that, I'd felt it was cruel, but now it seemed the decision was justified.

Colt left to finish his shift but promised to come back later to help with whatever we needed. Velma was coming by after she closed up, Nikki and Tanner would be staying to help out once they returned from Portland, and Lacy and Lonnie had both promised to come by as soon as they dropped off the kids with Lacy's parents. Velma had mentioned that Charlee was going to come by as well, so I figured we'd have more than enough hands to do whatever we needed. Deciding to have a selection of beers and soft drinks on ice for our helpers when they arrived, I headed over to the main house. When I entered through the back door, I heard Georgia talking to someone.

"Trish." I held out my arms in greeting. "I didn't think you would be here until this afternoon."

"I caught an earlier flight. I figured you girls could use some help and I wanted to pitch in."

"That is so nice of you." I hugged her.

"The place looks great. Georgia was just telling me about the flowers and tablecloths, but it seems as if you have things handled."

I nodded. "We do, but we are always happy for more help. Will you be able to stay long?"

"I'll be in town for a few days. I want to do more research while I'm here, especially because I feel like things are really coming together. I can't believe Emily turned out to be a dog, although I have to say, the story of the dog who died mourning her master was almost sadder than the one of Emily being a baby who died during or shortly after birth. Is that odd? It is odd. Right? I mean, why should I feel more empathy for the tragic death of a dog than I do for the tragic death of a baby who was never given a chance at life?"

I wrinkled my brow. "I will admit I felt the same way. At least initially. Then, once I thought about it, I felt grief not only for Emily and Elizabeth but for Elizabeth's entire family. It seems as if the Chestertons had a tough go of it. First, they lost

Elizabeth and then not all that many years later they lost Abagail. I can't even imagine how difficult it must have been for their parents."

Trish bowed her head. "I have found so much joy in learning about the lives of those who came before me, but there have been a lot of heart-wrenching moments as well. For every ancestor who had an amazing life, there has been one who suffered unimaginable tragedy. I suppose that is the way life goes, but I never expected to experience the ups and downs I have when I started this journey."

"If you had it to do all over again, would you?" Georgia asked.

"Absolutely."

Chapter 16

The day of the grand opening dawned bright and sunny. The air was still, the sky a deep, cloudless blue, and the sea mellow, with only the smallest of waves rolling toward the shore. My volunteers and I had worked late into the evening to get everything ready, but by the time they went home, everything was absolutely perfect.

Georgia was busy in the kitchen preparing the food that couldn't be made ahead of time. The mild temperature made it pleasant in both the sun and the shade as if an influence from above had a hand in things. The ads and flyers we'd created indicated that the doors to the inn would be open from two until after dark, but I suspected there might be a few early arrivals, so I wanted to do my last-minute chores and then get into the shower so I was ready to greet them.

I glanced down at Molly, who was staring up at me with hope in her eyes. "Would you like to take a short walk along the bluff?"

She barked once to indicate that she would.

I grabbed a tall cup of coffee and called to Ramos as well. The inn and grounds would be busy for most of the day, but at this moment in the early hours, it was just the animals and me. Rufus followed us out the door, so it was the four of us who greeted the day. I thought I might be frantic at this point, but the reality was, I was eerily calm. Georgia and I had worked hard, as had Lonnie and his crew, and after months and months of hard labor and hours of indecision, everything had finally come together almost exactly as I'd dreamed it would.

I paused and looked out at the sea. Seagulls flew overhead, searching for their morning meal. There were several fishing trawlers heading toward the horizon, hoping for a bountiful day at sea. I'd just turned to head back toward the cottage when my phone rang.

"Good morning," Lacy greeted me cheerily.

"Good morning to you too," I responded.

"Lonnie and I are going to drop the kids at his parents and then we'll be by to do whatever you need. Do you need us to stop to pick anything up? Lonnie's parents live in town, so it won't be out of the way."

"I think we are good, but you might check with Georgia. I'm out walking the pets right now, but she is back at the inn, cooking up a storm."

"Okay, I'll call her." Lacy paused to remind one of her sons to bring swim trunks because his grandparents planned to take them swimming at the community pool. "Listen, I need to go. The boys seem to have forgotten everything I just told them. Lonnie and I will be there in a couple of hours. If you think of anything you need, call me."

"I will. And thanks. I could never have done this without the two of you."

"We were thrilled to take this journey with you," Lacy responded.

"Be sure to bring business cards for both you and Lonnie. I'm sure once everyone gets a look at the remodel and the refurbished furniture, you will both be as busy as you want to be."

"That would be great." Lacy let out a breath. "Doing the sort of work Lonnie and I do can be a feast-or-famine situation much of the time. With six kids to feed, the times of famine can get dicey."

I signed off with Lacy and continued back toward the cottage. I figured once I got there I'd feed the animals, check in with Georgia, maybe take a walk through the garden to check for any weeds that might need eradicating, and then go back to the cottage to get ready. I planned to wear white pants with a bright blue top that I felt mirrored the color of the sea on a perfectly clear day. I'd decided on flat white sandals over heels because I was certain I would be on my feet for hours and hours today.

"Something smells delicious," I said to Georgia after I'd fed the animals and joined her in the kitchen of the main house.

"I've got homemade rolls for the sandwiches in the oven. I tried to focus on food that could be made ahead of time so that I wouldn't end up spending the entire day in the kitchen; sandwiches, along with salads and other finger foods seemed to fit the bill. I forgot to pick up the ice for the drinks, though, so Lonnie and Lacy are going to stop to pick some up on their way over. They should be here shortly."

"I just spoke to Lacy a little while ago. I guess the band members will be here early to set up as well."

Georgia nodded. "Lonnie said around noon. Nikki and the friends who are helping her to serve will be here by one, and Velma is taking the day off from the diner today to help me in the kitchen."

"Do you need my help with anything?"

Georgia looked around. "I think I'm good."

I was glad that Georgia had things handled but having nothing to do left me feeling restless. I headed out for my tour of the garden and then went back to the cottage to shower and dress. When I got out of the shower, I noticed I had a missed call from Colt. I pulled on a robe and called him back. I almost hoped he'd have questions about one of the investigations he was currently working on, but as it turned out, the reason he'd called was to let me know that the FBI had managed to track down Scarlett and he was waiting to hear from them, so he might be slightly later than he'd anticipated.

"Where did they find her?" I asked.

"LAX. She was trying to board a plane for Argentina. I'm waiting for a full report, but based on what I was told by the agent in charge, she tried to deny any wrongdoing when she was first detained, but once the agent who was interrogating her made it clear that Jeffery had talked, she began to cooperate as well."

"Did she say whether it was Evan Trout who killed Lora?"

"She admitted that. She was willing to indicate that she may have persuaded him to do it, which makes her as guilty as he is."

"And Peter?" I asked. "Where did he fit into it?"

"I'm not sure. At least not yet. I hope to know more by the time I see you this afternoon. Trout is in Argentina now, which is why Scarlett was heading there. The FBI is working with law enforcement in that country to have him apprehended." Colt paused to say something to someone in the background. "Listen, I have to go. I'll be at your place as soon as I can get there."

With that, he hung up.

I was glad that Colt had managed to figure out most of what had happened when Lora died. We now knew that Peter most likely had been in Atlanta when she was murdered and that it was Scarlett's friend who had killed her. Evan Trout had buried her in the forest not far from where he lived, and at some point, he had passed off Lora's cell phone to Scarlett, who must have been close at hand then. Jeffery and Scarlett both had benefited from Sophia's death, although it didn't appear as if Jeffery had actually gotten his hands dirty by being directly involved in her murder. The only thing we still didn't know was whether Peter knew about the plan to murder his wife and cooperated with Scarlett and Trout in any way. It was possible that he had honestly believed his wife was simply away, visiting a friend.

By the time Lonnie and Lacy arrived, I was dressed and ready to go. Lacy helped Georgia with some last-minute tasks while Lonnie greeted the band members and helped to get everything set up and organized. Nikki and Tanner showed up shortly after, with Velma right on their heels. When the first of the guests wandered in, everything was ready. Georgia and I greeted each one as they arrived. We spent the next several hours giving tours and making sure that everyone had all the food and drink they desired.

The event was well into its second hour when I paused to look out over the crowd. As happy as I was that everything had worked out just as I had imagined I knew my joy wouldn't be complete until Annie arrived.

"She'll be here," Georgia assured me, squeezing my arm in a show of support, even though I hadn't told her what I was thinking. Georgia always seemed to know.

"I know," I said, although the butterflies in my stomach seemed to say otherwise. "Annie always was one to want to make an entrance. I'm sure she'll be along at any moment." I glanced at Lacy, who was chatting with Tessa. "I think I'll head over to say hi to Tessa. I want to tell her that Molly has fit right in and can be assured of a loving family with which to spend her final years."

"Wow, this place is so great," Tessa said as I approached.

"Thank you. Georgia and I are really excited about it. Of course, the real work of running an inn is still ahead of us, but we're excited to get started."

"I think you are going to be a huge success. Everyone is talking about how gorgeous your suites are. You truly outdid yourselves."

"Most of the credit for the suites goes to Lonnie. Not only did he and his crew do all the work but the idea for the basic layout came from him as well."

"I've been thinking of remodeling my kitchen. I'll have to have a chat with him before I go." Tessa looked around at the crowd. "How is Molly doing?"

"She is doing great. She fits right in with my little ragtag family. Ramos absolutely adores her, and even Rufus is fine with her presence as long as she remembers which pillows belong to him."

Tessa smiled. "I am so thrilled that you and Molly found each other. I have to admit I was afraid that things were going to work out very differently for her."

I chatted with Tessa for a few more minutes before excusing myself to provide a tour for a group of new arrivals. When I returned to the patio, Colt was there, chatting with Tanner. I headed in their direction. "You made it. Did you get everything wrapped up?" I asked.

Colt nodded. "Once Scarlett started talking, she pretty much spilled the beans about everything, including that Peter really had no idea what was going on. He'd called Lora a couple of times after I'd contacted him at the conference about the report Erica had called in. Scarlett answered Lora's cell and pretended to be his estranged wife. Scarlett told the interrogator that she made it clear to Peter that their marriage was over and that she was leaving him and wouldn't be home when he got there. I guess initially he bought Scarlett's story because his marriage had been all but over, and that bought Scarlett and Trout some time. When Peter eventually became suspicious and began to question things, Scarlett had him killed as well."

"So she should be spending a good amount of time in prison."

"It looks that way."

"And Trout?"

Colt smiled. "He has been located. As Scarlett had informed the FBI, he was waiting for her in Argentina. He is currently in custody and will be extradited. According to Scarlett, only he knows where Peter is buried, but it appears that he is going to talk, so we should be able to recover his remains as well."

I shook my head. "I still can't believe that two people are dead because a greedy woman with no moral compass decided that money was more important than the lives of her sister and her sister's husband."

"It really is a tragedy. I'm just happy I could finally put the case to rest. I know that Erica has been unhappy about the fact that more wasn't done to find Lora's killer ever since it first happened."

"I guess it would be hard if you knew something to be true but no one believed you." I glanced out over the crowd. "Is Jeffery still in jail?"

"For now. He is cooperating and didn't actually kill anyone, so I imagine his sentence will be much lighter than the ones Scarlett and Trout are looking at."

"It looks like Lonnie is waving you over," I said.

Colt lifted an arm and waved back. "I told him I'd sit in for a set or two." He hugged me. "Enjoy your party. We'll catch up later."

After Colt went to join Lonnie and the band, I stood off to the side and considered what I had created. Not just a romantic and enchanting inn that I was sure was going to bring many lovely people into my life, but a family who meant more to me than I could say. I'd never really had a best friend. Not in the way Georgia was my best friend now. And Lonnie and Lacy were about as special to me as any friends had ever been. Nikki and Tanner were the best neighbors anyone could ever ask for, and Velma was almost like a mother to me. And Colt…well, I wasn't sure where Colt fit into things, but I did know he fit into my future somehow. Yet with all I had and everything I anticipated for the future, there was still a corner of my heart that could only be filled by one person.

"She's here," Georgia whispered in my ear, joining me at the edge of the lawn.

I looked toward the rear entrance of the inn. My heart skipped a beat when I saw Annie standing with Arnie on the deck, looking out over a sea of people. I slowly started forward until we stood face-to-face. "You came."

Annie nodded. "I said I would."

I stepped forward and wrapped my arms around her slight frame. At first, she stood stiffly, not hugging me back, so I hugged her harder. Eventually, I felt her arms tentatively wrap themselves around my body. I held on tight, not wanting to ever let go. When Annie tightened her hold rather than stepping away, the corner of my heart I knew only she could fill expanded until it burst with a happiness I hadn't felt since Ben and Johnathan had left me alone in a world that seemed too dark to navigate.

UP NEXT FROM KATHI DALEY BOOKS

https://amzn.to/2WrcrHn

PREVIEW:

Tuesday, October 22

The best stories, I've learned with time, seem to exist within the crossroads of fact and fiction.

"Welcome, everyone," I greeted the group of men and women who had shown up for the Tuesday night Mystery Lovers Book Club. "I'm thrilled to see so many new faces in the crowd. My name is Caitlin Hart West." It still felt odd using my new married surname. I glanced to my left. "This is my best friend and business partner of Tara O'Brian. We would both like to welcome our guest speaker, Winifred Westminster, to Coffee Cat Books. Winnifred pens novels in a variety of genres, including true crime, thriller, and traditional mystery." I paused as the group applauded. "Winifred, who prefers to be referred to as Winnie, will be releasing a novel this Christmas. The novel is based on the very real-life murder of Amy Anderson, a Madrona Island native who died almost fifteen years ago." I paused to let that sink in. Tara and I had both gone to the same high school as Amy, although she'd been two years older, and we'd both been at the party following the homecoming game at which Amy died. To say that Amy Anderson's murder hit close to home was putting it mildly, and while I had mixed feelings about Winnie exploiting the tragedy, I knew our patrons would be interested in hearing what she had to say, so when she asked to make a stop at Coffee Cat Books during her prepublication publicity tour, Tara and I had decided to welcome her. "I am going to turn the floor over to Winnie," I continued, "but first, I'd like to remind everyone to hold their comments and questions until the end."

I stepped aside and Winifred took the stage, which was really just a slightly raised platform my husband, Cody West, had built for the occasion. We'd transformed the lounge of Coffee Cat Books, the bookstore/coffee bar/cat lounge Tara and I owned, into an auditorium of sorts for our very special speaker, who had gained the interest of readers from as far away as Seattle.

"Thank you for having me," Winnie said after taking the floor. "The story of Amy Anderson is one I have been working on for a very long time. Amy was a high school student here on the island when she was brutally murdered while attending a party following the homecoming game fifteen years ago. The death of this delightful girl hit the community hard, but I think it hit me harder than most because I'd first met Amy during a very difficult time in my own history, and her sunny disposition had helped me to move on and take a second chance on life."

Winnie paused before she continued. She seemed to be a good storyteller who understood the art of pacing. Eventually, she continued in a slightly lower tone of voice. "My story opens where many good mysteries begin, on a dark and stormy night, this one in October almost thirty years ago. I first came to this island after my dear husband, Vinnie, passed away unexpectedly. Twenty-two was much too young to be a widow, and I found myself not only heartbroken but completely lost and alone. I can still remember sitting in a dark house my first night on the island. A storm had rolled in and I watched in silence as the sky flashed with lightning and rain poured down over the angry sea."

Winnie took a sip of water and slowly looked around the room. It seemed she had much of the audience on the edge of their seats. "The house I'd rented for the summer was a large old thing. Not only were there two stories of living space but there was a finished attic, which some past resident had used for storage, and a dank and damp, unfinished basement. The wind pounded the structure as it blew in from the sea and the walls swayed under the force of it all. It entered my mind that the storm might very well bring the whole house down around me, but at the time, I didn't care. Death, I'd already decided, would be a welcome reprieve from the life I now envisioned for myself."

I couldn't imagine how difficult it must be to lose the person you most depended on. The person who was to play a starring role in your future. The person who gave that future meaning. I tried to imagine life without Cody, but all I could imagine was darkness and despair. I supposed I could understand how, in that moment, Winnie really hadn't cared if she lived or died. I supposed that in a similar situation I might not either. But Winnie had survived and thrived, and I guess I knew that if forced to face a life of darkness, I would find my way back to the light as well.

Winnie continued. "I remember grieving for everything I had lost as the storm battered the island. I remember wondering if I had the strength to endure another day. I remember holding the bottle of sedatives I had been prescribed and considering the options, when I heard a noise that sounded a lot like someone crying. I was sure I was alone in the house, but it sounded so real. I listened for a moment but couldn't tell what I was hearing, so I decided to take a look around. I began by exploring the main floor of living space, but when I didn't find anything that would explain the crying, I headed down the stairs to the basement, where I found a little girl who couldn't be more than four or five sitting in the middle of the unfinished room sobbing. I asked her who she was and how she had gotten there, and she shared that her name was Amy and that she had followed her cat into the basement through an air vent that led to the outside. I asked her why she was crying and she said that her cat had disappeared and she couldn't find the crawlspace leading to the small opening that would allow her to get out of the room. I'd just moved in and wasn't aware of an exterior access point, so I picked up the child, took her upstairs, and then carried her to the house next door, where her mother was baking. The poor woman was a mess when she found out that Amy wasn't upstairs taking a nap as she'd thought. She offered me a cup of tea and we got to talking, and suddenly the dark and empty space that had been my life since Vinnie died seemed a little brighter. From that moment, I knew I'd found a surrogate family of sorts. At least for the summer. Amy was such a cute little thing. She would come over to my house to visit with me, sometimes bringing flowers she'd picked from her mother's garden. I wasn't normally much of a baker, but that summer I always made sure I had plenty of homemade cookies for Amy when she came by."

"So what happened?" one of the women in the audience asked. "After that summer?"

"I returned to my old life. When I'd arrived on Madrona Island, I'd been a broken woman, but after the long summer here, and the companionship of this very special little girl, I felt ready to rebuild the life I'd left behind. I came back to the island the following summer and a few times after that, but then I published my first book and began to spend time developing my career. My visits became shorter and less frequent, and eventually, my life as a writer took over and I stopped coming altogether. I usually remembered to send Amy a card for her birthday, and I made a point of sending a package around the holidays, but I will admit we lost touch as the years went by. I'm sure my relationship with the child I'd found on that rainy day would have faded into a distant memory if left to decay naturally over time, but then I learned of Amy's brutal death, and what had been a warm and pleasant memory turned into something dark and filled with rage."

"Who killed her? And why?" another of the women asked.

"I didn't know for a very long time. No one did. But then I came to the island a year and a half ago to spend some time with my thoughts after my life became hectic once again. I happened to run into a woman I'd met when I'd visited the island all those years ago and we got to talking. She mentioned something about Amy and the events leading up to her death, which got me to thinking. I latched onto an idea that had popped into my head and began to dig around a bit. Eventually, I stumbled on to something that led me to the answer I'd been seeking. Once I began to puzzle things through, I realized I'd happened across a clue, which then led to another clue, which finally led to the answer that seemed to have been there just waiting all along."

"So who did it? Who killed Amy?" the woman asked once again.

"If you want the answer to that question, you will need to read the book."

I had a feeling that Winnie was going to sell a lot of books. Not only had the presentation she'd provided for our customers been completely captivating but if she had solved the murder, I knew that everyone, including the resident deputy, my brother-in-law, Ryan Finnegan, was going to be interested in learning the answer no one had been able to find to this point.

"So you figured out who killed Amy and haven't told anyone?" The same woman appeared to be beyond shocked.

Winnie bobbed her head. "As I've already said, the answer to the question of who murdered Amy Anderson will be revealed when the book is published."

"But you are giving the killer time to get away," the woman insisted.

I found I had to agree with that, but while Winnie was willing to answer questions after her presentation, she refused to give away the ending of her book no matter how many people asked. In a way, I could see why she would want to keep that to herself until the book was published, but it seemed wrong to me that she had figured out the answer to a fifteen-year-old old murder yet hadn't shared that information with anyone, including Amy's parents and law enforcement.

After everyone left, Tara and I began cleaning up.

"So, what did you make of the presentation?" she asked as the first of many raindrops began to hit the wall of windows that overlooked the dark sea.

"Winnie certainly is a good storyteller and she seemed to be able to draw every single person in the room into her tale, but I do wonder how she solved a murder no one has been able to figure out in the past fifteen years."

Tara folded one of the chairs and added it to the stack to return to the storage room. "Yeah. I did find myself wondering about the specifics of the whole thing. I mean, if she has identified the killer, shouldn't she have at the very least told Finn what she knows? And even if she didn't want Finn to ruin her big reveal, doesn't it seem dangerous to taunt the killer with the fact that he or she has been identified and it is only a matter of time before their secret is known?"

"It does seem as if she is traveling a dangerous road," I agreed.

"When Winnie asked to speak to our club, I knew she had been working on a novel based on the story of Amy's death, but I had no idea she'd actually solved the murder," Tara said. "I wonder if Finn knows."

"I guess we can ask him. Siobhan mentioned that they had a babysitter and she and Finn were going to O'Malley's for dinner and drinks," I said, referring to my older sister. "They might still be there."

O'Malley's was the bar my two brothers, Aiden and Danny, had bought and refurbished.

"I wouldn't mind a drink," Tara said.

"Cody is in Florida with his mother until tomorrow, so I have no reason to hurry home. If Winnie really has figured out what happened to Amy and isn't just making this whole thing up to sell more books, I would think Finn would insist that she share that information with him."

"I'm not sure he can force her to tell him anything she has dug up, but there is the whole withholding evidence thing they always talk about on the cop shows I enjoy on TV, so maybe. Let's finish up here and then head to O'Malley's. I wanted to talk to Danny anyway. He wants to throw a Halloween party at the bar and asked me if I would help him with the food and decorations."

"It's nice of you to help."

Tara shrugged. "I don't mind, and he is letting us use the bar for the party following the homecoming game on Saturday. It seems that a lot of alumni plan to be in town this year. It will be good to catch up with everyone."

"I was talking to Owen Nelson about doing a photo of my cabin for the wall over the fireplace in the new house, and he mentioned that Archie planned to be in town this year." Owen Nelson had been introverted and socially awkward in high school and had never really fit in with the popular crowd. He hadn't been supersmart like his friends, but he had been a talented photographer who'd worked on both the yearbook and the school newspaper. He went on to open his own photography studio after school and seemed to be doing very well. His best friends in high school had been Archie Baldwin, a computer geek who went on to work for the NSA, and Becky Bollinger, another computer geek, who went on to own a major software company. Both Archie and Becky had moved off the island after graduation.

"Is Becky coming as well?" Tara asked. In high school, Owen, Archie, and Becky, had been inseparable. Most referred to them as the Three Nerdsketeers.

"He wasn't sure. He hoped Becky could make it, but her software company has grown a lot over the past two years, so she is pretty busy."

"I heard she is doing really well. I hope she can make it. It would be fun to catch up. We need to be sure to get the word out about the party at the bar. Owen, Archie, and Becky were in Danny and Cody's class, but I'm going to be sure to invite those alumni who are still around from our class as well." Tara began turning off the lights. "I've heard they are expecting to have a good turnout for the game this year."

"I've noticed that homecoming games played in October have a better turnout than the ones in September. I've also noticed that alumni are more apt to come back for the first few games after graduation, but then their attendance tapers off." I checked to make sure the coffee machines were cleaned and ready for the morning. "It will be good to see whoever shows."

As soon as Tara and I finished cleaning up, we headed to the bar. Weekdays in the off-season tended to be slow, so other than a few regulars sitting at the bar, the place was mostly empty. Finn and Siobhan were sitting at the far end of the long, horseshoe-shaped bar, chatting with Danny and Aiden, so Tara and I joined them.

"How was the author presentation?" Siobhan asked as I slid onto a stool next to her.

"Interesting." I leaned in a bit so I could see Finn, who was sitting on her other side. "Winnie Westminster told the group that she had solved the Amy Anderson murder and would reveal the killer in her new book."

Finn frowned. "That sounds like a bad idea."

"That's what I thought. I feel like she is practically daring the killer to take action before she is able to make the big reveal."

"Do you know where she is staying?" Finn asked.

"She rented a house on the west shore, just north of Harthaven. It is the same house she rented when she met Amy when she was a child. Amy's family no longer lives in the house next door, and Winnie didn't mention an address, but I'm sure you can figure it out if you want to have a chat with her."

"I have the address in my file." Finn looked at Siobhan. "I hate to cut our evening short, but do you mind getting a ride home with Cait?"

"Happy to. If it turns out that you are going to be longer than an hour or two, text me to let me know what's going on."

Finn leaned forward and kissed his wife. "I will." He looked at me. "How long has Ms. Wesminster been on the island?"

"I think she just arrived yesterday."

"And had you heard, prior to this evening, that the woman was claiming to have solved the Amy Anderson murder case?"

I shook my head. "No. I did know she had written a book based on Amy and her death, but until she said so this evening, I had no idea that she was actually identifying the killer."

"So maybe the killer hasn't heard that potentially dangerous information either."

I shrugged. "Maybe not. Unless the killer was at the meeting tonight. We've been advertising the fact that Winifred Westminster was going to be a guest at Coffee Cat Books for the past several weeks, and our ads did indicate that she had written a book about the Amy Anderson murder. If I was the killer and I still lived in the area, I might show up to hear what she had to say."

Finn narrowed his gaze. "I'll see if I can get Winifred to share what she knows for her own safety." He looked at Siobhan. "I'll call you after I get a feel for how things are going to go."

After Finn left, Tara, Siobhan, and I moved to a table. Aiden stayed behind the bar, but Danny joined us.

"I have to admit that Winnie's talk tonight brought up a lot of really weird emotions that I suppose I've been suppressing for years," Tara said.

"I know what you mean," I agreed. "The fact that Amy was murdered in a house filled with dozens of people and not a single person even knew she was dead until her body was found the next morning is beyond strange. It seems to me that she would have screamed if she was being attacked. If she did, you would think someone would have heard her."

"The music was loud that night," Danny pointed out.

"Maybe, but there must have been a struggle. It just seems unlikely to me that not a single person heard what was going on."

"I seem to remember that Amy was pretty drunk," Tara said. "Maybe she went upstairs and passed out. Someone could have killed her while she was out. She may not have even been aware of what was happening until it was too late to scream."

I picked up my wine and took a sip. "I suppose it could have happened that way." I knew Amy's body had been found on top of the bed in Lance's parent's bedroom the morning after the party. The medical examiner had determined that she'd died at around eleven p.m., but apparently, no one had realized Amy was missing until the next day.

"I wonder if Amy was drugged," Tara suggested. "I won't say I knew Amy well, but from what I did know of her, she didn't seem the sort to drink until she passed out."

"She wasn't really herself that night," Danny said. "If you remember, she'd just broken up with Brock, who had showed up at the party with Jamie."

Brock Stevenson had dated Amy all through high school, and I did remember that Amy took it hard when he broke up with her. Brock had brought a girl named Jamie Fisher to the party that night. Jaime and Amy were both popular cheerleaders and most kids considered them to be rivals. "I remember that when

Amy saw Jaime with Brock she did not take it well, so I suppose that Brock showing up with Jamie might explain why she got so drunk, but it doesn't explain who killed her."

Siobhan had been listening, but she had already graduated and left the island by the time of the party, so she didn't really know any of the people we were discussing. When her phone buzzed, she picked it up and stepped away to take the call. Danny, Tara, and I continued to discuss possible suspects. Once we got to tossing around names, we came up with a fairly long list.

I glanced up as Siobhan returned to the table with a huge frown on her face. "What's wrong?"

"That was Finn. When he arrived at the house Winnifred was renting, he found the front door partially open. When she didn't answer his knock he let himself in. He found her dead on the living room floor."

"Dead?" I gasped.

Books by Kathi Daley

Come for the murder, stay for the romance.

Zoe Donovan Cozy Mystery:

Halloween Hijinks
The Trouble With Turkeys
Christmas Crazy
Cupid's Curse
Big Bunny Bump-off
Beach Blanket Barbie
Maui Madness
Derby Divas
Haunted Hamlet
Turkeys, Tuxes, and Tabbies
Christmas Cozy
Alaskan Alliance
Matrimony Meltdown
Soul Surrender
Heavenly Honeymoon
Hopscotch Homicide
Ghostly Graveyard
Santa Sleuth
Shamrock Shenanigans
Kitten Kaboodle
Costume Catastrophe
Candy Cane Caper
Holiday Hangover
Easter Escapade
Camp Carter
Trick or Treason
Reindeer Roundup
Hippity Hoppity Homicide

Firework Fiasco
Henderson House
Holiday Hostage
Lunacy Lake
Celtic Christmas – *December 2019*

Zimmerman Academy The New Normal
Zimmerman Academy New Beginnings
Ashton Falls Cozy Cookbook

Tj Jensen Paradise Lake Mysteries
Pumpkins in Paradise
Snowmen in Paradise
Bikinis in Paradise
Christmas in Paradise
Puppies in Paradise
Halloween in Paradise
Treasure in Paradise
Fireworks in Paradise
Beaches in Paradise
Thanksgiving in Paradise – *Fall 2019*

Writers' Retreat Mystery:
First Case
Second Look
Third Strike
Fourth Victim
Fifth Night
Sixth Cabin
Seventh Chapter
Eighth Witness
Ninth Grave

Whales and Tails Cozy Mystery:

Romeow and Juliet
The Mad Catter
Grimm's Furry Tail
Much Ado About Felines
Legend of Tabby Hollow
Cat of Christmas Past
A Tale of Two Tabbies
The Great Catsby
Count Catula
The Cat of Christmas Present
A Winter's Tail
The Taming of the Tabby
Frankencat
The Cat of Christmas Future
Farewell to Felines
A Whisker in Time
The Catsgiving Feast
A Whale of a Tail

Rescue Alaska Mystery:

Finding Justice
Finding Answers
Finding Courage
Finding Christmas
Finding Shelter – *Fall 2019*

The Inn at Holiday Bay:

Boxes in the Basement
Letters in the Library
Message in the Mantel
Answers in the Attic
Haunting in the Hallway – *Fall 2019*

A Tess and Tilly Mystery:

The Christmas Letter
The Valentine Mystery
The Mother's Day Mishap
The Halloween House
The Thanksgiving Trip
The Saint Paddy's Promise
The Halloween Haunting – *Fall 2019*

The Hathaway Sisters:

Harper
Harlow
Hayden – *Summer 2019*

Haunting by the Sea:

Homecoming by the Sea
Secrets by the Sea
Missing by the Sea
Betrayal by the Sea
Christmas by the Sea – *Winter 2019*

Sand and Sea Hawaiian Mystery:

Murder at Dolphin Bay
Murder at Sunrise Beach
Murder at the Witching Hour
Murder at Christmas
Murder at Turtle Cove
Murder at Water's Edge
Murder at Midnight
Murder at Pope Investigations – *Summer 2019*

Seacliff High Mystery:

The Secret
The Curse
The Relic
The Conspiracy
The Grudge
The Shadow
The Haunting

Road to Christmas Romance:

Road to Christmas Past

USA Today best-selling author Kathi Daley lives in beautiful Lake Tahoe with her husband Ken. When she isn't writing, she likes spending time hiking the miles of desolate trails surrounding her home. She has authored more than a hundred books in eleven series, including Zoe Donovan Cozy Mysteries, Whales and Tails Island Mysteries, Tess and Tilly Cozy Mysteries, Sand and Sea Hawaiian Mysteries, Tj Jensen Paradise Lake Series, Inn at Holiday Bay Cozy Mysteries, Writers' Retreat Southern Seashore Mysteries, Rescue Alaska Paranormal Mysteries, Haunting by the Sea Paranormal Mysteries, Family Ties Mystery Romances, and Seacliff High Teen Mysteries. Find out more about her books at www.kathidaley.com

Stay up-to-date:
Newsletter, *The Daley Weekly*
http://eepurl.com/NRPDf
Webpage – www.kathidaley.com
Facebook at Kathi Daley Books –
www.facebook.com/kathidaleybooks
Kathi Daley Books Group Page –
https://www.facebook.com/groups/569578823146850/
E-mail – kathidaley@kathidaley.com
Twitter at Kathi Daley@kathidaley –
https://twitter.com/kathidaley
Amazon Author Page –
https://www.amazon.com/author/kathidaley
BookBub –
https://www.bookbub.com/authors/kathi-daley